ABOUT THE AUTHOR

Aleksandr Skorobogatov [illegible] a small Belorussian town [illegible] Poland. His novels have been published to great acclaim in Russian, Croatian, Danish, Dutch, French, Italian, Greek, Serbian and Spanish. In 1991 *Russian Gothic* won the 'Best Novel of the Year' award from *Yunost'* in Russia; the Italian edition won the prestigious International Literary Award Città di Penne. Skorobogatov lives and works in Belgium, where the newspaper *De Tijd* has called him 'the best Russian writer of the moment'.

SELECTED PRAISE FOR *RUSSIAN GOTHIC*

'Sublime and breathtaking' *Lektuurgids*

'Heart-rending realism' *Nouvel Observateur*

'A thrilling novel about guilt and atonement' *De Volkskrant*

'What writers like Dostoyevsky, Chekhov, and Gogol did over a century ago, Skorobogatov now does in a modern guise, giving shape to the Russian soul in a story about love and revenge.' *Noord Hollands Dagblad*

First published in Russia in 1991

This edition published in 2023 by

Old Street Publishing
Notaries House, Devon EX1 1AJ
www.oldstreetpublishing.co.uk

ISBN 978-1-91040-090-6

10 9 8 7 6 5 4 3 2 1

A CIP catalogue record for this title is available from the British Library.

Printed and bound in the United Kingdom

RUSSIAN GOTHIC

ALEKSANDR SKOROBOGATOV

TRANSLATED BY ILONA YAZHBIN CHAVASSE

For my beloved daughters,
Katrien and Liza

They say he murdered women, using a short-bladed knife with a crooked bone handle to rip open their bellies, and then burrowed his feet inside. He liked to wiggle his toes in there, but he didn't like it at all when the women screamed. They say that happened sometimes, when he didn't kill them straight away. Then he would grow angry and his pleasure was quite ruined. Yet this was rare, very rare. After all, he was good at killing people, a master of his craft.

They say he called himself for some reason Sergeant Bertrand; a peculiar name. They say he was arrested and executed by firing squad, but I've also heard that as he walked down the gloomy tunnel towards his death, towards the firing squad with their pre-war rifles, he vanished. They heard his heavy footsteps reverberating in the dark, and then nothing – they suddenly stopped, as though the Sergeant had stopped walking. There was nowhere to hide in that tunnel, and yet he was never found. He had vanished – the man who called himself Sergeant Bertrand.

But it's also possible, and this is much more likely, that he never existed at all, this person whom others for some reason had named Sergeant Bertrand even though he already had a name of his own...

Surely he must have had a name? What was it?

SERGEANT BERTRAND

When did it begin? Nikolai could no longer say for sure. Perhaps one evening the front door had swung open and the man simply strolled in. Smiling calmly, he took off his hat and kissed the hand of Nikolai's wife, before making his way over to Nikolai himself. He greeted Nikolai like an old friend, sat on the chair beside his bed and peered at him with a solemn sort of sympathy. For some reason it occurred to Nikolai that this would be precisely how the Sergeant would appear at his, Nikolai's, funeral – solemn and concerned. Yes, that was what Nikolai thought the very first time Bertrand came into his room.

Or perhaps it hadn't happened that way at all. On the contrary, maybe they had been having breakfast, and Vera had just brought in the teapot, a little cloud of steam escaping the spout with each step she took. In front of Nikolai was a plateful of fried eggs (along with pinkish tomato wedges, pinkish slices of fried sausage, needle-like sprigs of dill) and a shot of vodka, just poured and still trembling in a pretty, gold-rimmed shot glass. Vera bent down to kiss Nikolai's head. He nodded, knocked back the vodka with a violent tilt of the head, exhaled noisily, and then, hunching low over his plate as always, forked the first bit of egg.

At that moment the doorbell rang. It went on for some time.

'Doorbell,' he said. It seemed Vera hadn't heard.

'What did you say?'

'Someone's ringing the doorbell,' repeated Nikolai, irritated.

'Oh, sorry,' said his wife. 'I was miles away. I'll go and open the door – you eat.'

Vera sprang lightly to her feet and ran out into the corridor. He heard the click of the lock and then whispers. If she'd spoken normally, chances are Nikolai wouldn't have pricked up his ears, would never have wondered who was at the door, and why. But Vera was whispering, and that told him right away that she wished to conceal the conversation from him.

On tiptoes, still grasping his fork, Nikolai crept to the entrance hall. With each step the whispering grew louder. As he neared the door, he began to make out some words. He heard Vera say, 'No, he's still at home,' and then, 'I'll phone once he's gone.' Who was she talking about? Who was 'at home' besides himself? And who was she planning to phone 'once he'd gone'? The door slammed shut and Nikolai hurried back to the table. He was out of breath. He poured himself another shot, spilling some vodka onto the tablecloth.

Vera came into the room and sat down again. She seemed more cheerful, as if the encounter at the door had pleasantly excited her.

'Who was it?' Nikolai asked casually, spearing an elusive bit of tomato, not looking at her.

'I don't know,' said Vera.

'What do you mean, you don't know?' Nikolai dropped his fork and turned towards her. 'You don't know who you were just speaking to?'

His wife looked at him in confusion. 'There was no one there... Maybe you just imagined it? Or it could have been kids? You know, they ring the doorbell then run away.'

'But I heard...'

Nikolai cut himself short. It would be a mistake to admit he had actually heard her whispering with someone.

'What did you hear?'

'Nothing.'

He went to the front door and listened: the sound of unhurried footsteps descending. Quietly, trying not to let the lock click, he opened the door and peered over the railings down the stairwell. He couldn't see the owner of the footsteps. There was a smell of burning. Nikolai glanced back towards the door – Vera was watching him with frightened eyes from the hallway – then raced down the stairs, trying to make as little noise as possible. The heavy front door slammed. On the first-floor landing Nikolai paused; the staircase below him was empty. He ran down the last flight, shoved open the front door and raced outside. Bright daylight momentarily blinded him. Thick black smoke billowed from the large communal trash container: the trash was burning. The stench made Nikolai's stomach heave. The yard was empty, but out of the corner of his eye Nikolai saw someone disappear behind the trash container. Chasing after the figure, he ran straight into the suffocating cloud of black smoke and was forced to shut his eyes and hold his breath. When he emerged and opened his eyes again there was no one there. He stood scanning the yard, then ran to investigate the stairwell of the next-door building, the one nearest the container with its smouldering heap of leather or rubber or whatever it was – but that was empty too. So was the next-door yard, except for some boys kicking about a flaccid rubber football. Their snot-nosed goalkeeper kept fiddling uselessly with his ragged, over-sized leather gloves. Beyond that was the road and the rush of passing cars. A bus was pulling away from the stop and an old lady with a bagful of sprouted potatoes stared at Nikolai with complete indifference, just standing there barefoot by the side of the road. He almost burst into tears on the way home.

'What's wrong?' Vera asked sympathetically, meeting him in the hall. She tried to run a hand through his hair. 'Are you feeling ill?'

'I'm feeling fine,' he said, flicking her hand away, and went straight to his room, slamming the door behind him.

'I'm feeling just wonderful,' he said in the bedroom, where he collapsed onto the bed and covered his face with his hands – just as their young son had done when he was overcome by childish tears and trying to hide them – and as he, Nikolai, always did when he felt upset and frightened and tired of living and only wanted one thing, one simple thing, to die there and then, that very second, at once. It was absurd, he knew. After all, how could he die, leaving her all alone in the world?

***

Perhaps that was how Sergeant Bertrand first visited, while they were having breakfast. But Nikolai had his doubts. More likely, it had been in the evening. Nikolai remembered it was dark outside. He had been lying in bed with another headache, feeling queasy and too hot, unable to get comfortable under the covers. Vera was by herself in the living room, sitting at the table... yes, that's right... and then the doorbell rang.

Vera led Bertrand to the living room. They made sure that the door to Nikolai's room was tightly shut. Then Vera held out her hands to him, and Bertrand pressed them ardently to his lips.

BUTTERFLY

After that first time, Sergeant Bertrand became a frequent visitor. If Vera happened to be home, he'd walk over to her smiling and kiss her hand – many times, each and every finger, as though Vera were his wife – or rather, as it seemed to Nikolai, his mistress. Vera would smile back at him languidly – a look so familiar and so agonisingly dear to Nikolai – then she would tip back her head so that her neck could be admired. Sometimes she would half-close her eyes with the sweet torment of it, sweet and sharp all at once.

Bertrand was tall and upright: he never slouched. His movements were vigorous and brisk, as if premeditated and measured out in advance. His hair was cut very short, military-style. His eyes were sky blue and bottomless.

***

Even that very first time, Nikolai had been unpleasantly struck by the easy familiarity of Bertrand's kissing Vera's hands, completely unfazed by his presence. When he recalled that night, Nikolai couldn't fathom how it was that he hadn't got out of bed – and hadn't said a word about it to Bertrand since, never mind stopped them. Although to be fair, there was a simple explanation: it was Bertrand's first visit, and Nikolai felt awkward and embarrassed. It would cause a scandal, he would have to shout, even fight. With a man visiting for the first time, a guest...

***

The next morning his first thought was of the smile he had seen on his wife's face. Vera had not been able to restrain herself after giving both her hands to Bertrand, even though she knew perfectly well that Nikolai was in the next room and could easily be watching from behind the door. She hadn't smiled like that at Nikolai for ages, though there was a time – before, oh God, before their son died – when it had been her usual smile. He almost never saw it these days, and then, only in the most intimate, secret moments of their life together. What was it about the faint, vague movement of her lips that stirred him so?

He was stunned by how brazenly Vera lied to him, to his face, feigning incomprehension at first, then pretending to be offended. With her face turned to the wall she would weep, her frail, naked shoulder trembling above the collar of her slipping nightgown. He had expected her to make excuses, to beg forgiveness, plead with him to forget her terrible mistake, never to be repeated, of course not, never, not for anything. God, what a lie it was, an endless stream of shameless lies... But he was fully prepared, once the necessary assurances had been made, to forgive, to forgive and even to believe again, because with all his heart he wanted to believe her, he so passionately wanted to believe her, so much that his heart broke in anticipation of the lies, and ridiculous as it sounds, he was, yes, heartsick... She only had to ask forgiveness and all would be forgiven, understood, forgotten – but no, none of that happened, instead of begging forgiveness she insisted that no one had visited during the previous evening, that she didn't know anyone called Bertrand, that nobody had kissed her hands, she had spent all evening reading by the table, she'd only stepped out once to look in on the lady next door... That's what it was called now, it seemed – 'looking in on the lady next door.' Well at least it was only once! That was something!

He apprehended her by the bathroom, her new favourite place to lock herself away and cry. Pulling her back to face him by her still bare shoulder – its inexpressible, provoking beauty pained him – he slapped her hard in the face, trying not to look her in the eyes. He knew they would be brimming with fear, tears, grief, and something else when she looked at him, but of course most of all fear – fear of another blow. The slap made a loud, ringing noise; she collapsed in the corner and perhaps burst into tears, hands shielding her face. She cowered on the floor very close to the bathroom door. What was she screaming? Really, though, did it make any difference? 'Don't, please, I'm begging you, don't!' Same old, same old. The standard repertoire.

Standing over her, he shouted that if this were to happen again, even once, if she ever again allowed Bertrand to kiss her hands – no, if she dared so much as to *give* him her hands, to hold them out to him – Nikolai would simply hurl them out of the house, the pair of them, and shame them in front of all the neighbours.

'I don't understand, I don't understand anything! What are you talking about?' cried Vera, and he could barely restrain himself from hitting her again. He only lifted her from the floor by her hair, gritting his teeth. She was so beautiful. He loved her so completely. If she could only see – for even a moment – his endless agony in loving her... He would die for her with the greatest joy. But she was not worthy of his love. It was beyond him to make her his alone.

His head hurt unbearably, terribly. In the time before, he remembered, headaches would come in fits, and sometimes the pain would depart as quickly as it arrived. After Vera had left for work, Nikolai couldn't clearly recollect whether he had beaten her or not. At any rate, that was the day he finally became certain of what he had long suspected: his wife was a sneaky, pathological slut. She was an actress, what else could you expect?

But no – he didn't think he had hit Vera that morning, after all. He remembered perfectly how he had wanted to hit her – yes, when he had caught her by the bathroom door – but he had held back, he told himself, so as not to frighten her away. So as not to frighten the butterfly away. But why had she been lying on the floor, and he, bending down, lifting her up, she in tears, her face wet, her eyes wet, ceaseless tears running down her face, one after another, as if each one was afraid of being left behind... and then her eyelashes, wet, black, stuck together... and in his palm, strands of her hair?

He hadn't hit her, and here's why: so as not to frighten her away. You need to approach a butterfly carefully, you mustn't let your shadow fall over it, you have to move smoothly. Even a look can scare a butterfly.

THE ZOO

Before long Bertrand was visiting daily, and sometimes several times a day. Radiant, gleaming with health, redolent of subtle and no doubt expensive perfume, he'd show himself in and saunter up to Vera, kissing – all but licking – her fingertips, before wandering over to Nikolai's room.

He never knocked. Instead he'd fling open the door and collapse onto the armchair, then take out a cigarette and light up. First he'd sit silently, silently inhaling, silently tapping ash into the ashtray, casting his eye over the room as if something might have changed in his absence.

'Why are you always sitting in the dark?' That was the kind of thing he might ask.

'It's how I like it,' Nikolai would reply.

Then Bertrand would fall silent again, and Nikolai never felt like talking anyway.

It was a special kind of torture when Vera came in to empty the overflowing ashtray and wipe the coating of ash off the table – or to ask, feigning concern, how he was feeling, how was his head, did he need anything, could she make him some tea, or take the empty bottle? There was always some excuse to flaunt herself before Bertrand, whom she pretended not to notice lounging in the armchair opposite Nikolai. Meanwhile, not in the least embarrassed by Nikolai's presence, Bertrand would follow her with his eyes, drinking her in, admiring her with no shame at all.

'What a strange, remarkable beauty!' Bertrand would

pronounce when Vera finally left the room. 'And what rare perfection of form! The way the bosom strains against the sweater, as though it hasn't enough room under there! You are in possession of a treasure... but treasures have a habit of slipping through your fingers. Or thieves get their hands on them!'

At this he would laugh, delighted with his pointless joke, too stupid to deserve the name and worn to death with repetition.

'Do you remember that strange old legend, about the queen who, for one night, gave her lover access to all her womanly charms, but only provided he agreed to be put to death in the morning? A highly improbable story, don't you think? But then you come across a woman whose beauty is more precious to you than the world, whose intimacy, no matter how short-lived, is worth your life – with all its countless joys and pleasures, all the conceivable meetings with inconceivably beautiful women, all the wonderful love affairs, and glorious ecstasies in the arms of other women, a life of far greater riches than a single tragi-romantic night. Naturally quite a few of the reckless lovers couldn't even do the deed, perhaps from thinking about their execution on the morrow, or else out of grief that the bliss – however long desired and, no doubt, infinitely piquant – would come to an end in the morning. Or maybe they shrank timidly from laying a finger on the cruel lady's 'sacred beauty'. Or else perhaps the more sensitive chaps just couldn't get it up, secretly afraid of disappointing she who had so graciously opened her legs for them... Needless to say, there were various reasons. Still, seriously – and I'm not just saying it – I'd pay through the nose for a woman like yours.'

Bertrand had a habit of licking his lips when saying such things; his mouth was always moist.

'But as for giving my life for her... I think not!'

This would always make him laugh long and heartily.

'You see, life is such an incredibly long, almost endless run of time... To barter it for a single night? And would it be as passionate a night as one had dreamed of? That is the question. But half my life, let's say – yes, I'd pay that almost without a qualm. When you think about it, isn't it strange that you should have been so lucky? A woman like that is beyond the wildest dreams of most men – yet here you are, and she's your very own, in your very own bed. Your wife. She belongs to you. You are a lucky devil, aren't you? Are you lucky at cards too? Unlucky at cards, lucky in love – isn't that what they say? What about the other way around?'

Nikolai lit a cigarette and began to pace the dark room. He poured himself some vodka and drank it slowly in small sips, through clenched teeth. But the vodka didn't always help; it all depended on how much he'd had before Bertrand's arrival.

And Bertrand kept on talking, endlessly talking, regarding Nikolai with a lazy, mocking air as he paced the short, narrow room from window to bed. How many steps was it? A single crossing took just five steps; the little room was barely five metres long. But over the course of an evening in Bertrand's company, there were many, so many... kilometres of steps...

Why do I put up with him? Once I took my son to the zoo, and there a wolf was loping up and down a tormentingly small cage: two blank walls, a third wall with an opening like the mouth of a cave, as if to replicate the wolf's natural home, and finally a row of bars painted brown (again natural colours) that completed the wolf's circumscribed world. The animal rushed at the bars, then quickly back to the opposite wall with its entrance to the fictitious lair, and so on, again and again, back and forth from bars to wall and back, bars to wall, as though training for some lupine contest, some wolfish marathon, unable to comprehend that it was all finished for him, his life was over and could never be recovered, and all he had left was the cage, and beyond it the curious visitors – like that young man here, for example, the one with a long scar down his forehead, the one with a little boy – still a very little boy, who gazed at the terrible, wild, fanged, clawed, real-life big bad wolf, his bright innocent eyes shining with equal parts terror and delight. In the next-door cage was an even more pathetic creature, some sort of idiotic raccoon, who stood on his hind legs and rubbed the thick steel bars with his front paws, very quickly and with barely a pause. In those places the bars were not only polished to a steely gleam but also noticeably thinner. Foolish creature, with its naïve hope of outwitting its fate, of wearing through those bars and fleeing the hospitality of the zoological gardens, sneaking off unseen into the deep wild woods... But what wild woods, when all this raccoon knew was to stand behind bars and polish them with his front paws – that and to guzzle the meals in his feeder tray, meals specially prepared by the zoologists and which the zoo-keepers pilfered? How could it be that nature lovers had caught him in the wild, and torn him unthinkingly from his beloved?

'Do you know what a real woman wants?' Bertrand went on. 'A woman like yours, for instance? You think she wants some special virtues, like looks, or grace, or greatness of mind, talent, devotion, tenderness...? Don't be a fool. It's strength.' Bertrand made a fist. 'Strength. *A woman likes to feel brute force.* Just as we expect beauty of a woman, first and foremost, a real woman demands strength from her man. And naturally, above all in his trousers... Some women value that kind of muscle more than anything else!'

Bertrand paused, grinning, as though unsure whether to pronounce his next thought.

'You know what I'd do, if she were mine? I'd stroke her little legs, if she was mine, stroke them and nibble them... just nip them here and there, lightly, softly, tenderly. You can drive a sensuous woman to screams of pleasure, doing no more than that, to loss of consciousness, to the sweetest heights of...'

'Don't you dare say a word about her!' Nikolai halted near Bertrand's chair, his hand raised to strike. Sometimes Nikolai felt such hatred for the man, it made him light-headed. He stumbled, and collapsed shamefully to the floor, overturning both chair and table. No big deal – after all the ashtray was empty and there was no glassware on the table.

'You're drunk and your nerves are shot. And anyway, I don't mean any offence. If you were in any state to think rationally, you'd see that my worship of your wife is strictly platonic. I admire her beauty as any cultured person might, that's all – so get a grip.'

'I'm perfectly calm,' said Nikolai, rising painfully from the floor. He began to pace the room again, keeping time with the regular, heavy beat of the blood in his temples. His pulse was very slow, especially when he had been drinking. Or did it only seem that way?

When Bertrand had finished his cigarette, he spent a long time stubbing it out, then immediately started another with a click of his gold lighter. He rarely – almost never – inhaled, but for some reason he liked having a burning cigarette in his fingers.

VERA

Nikolai drew back the heavy curtain only when it was completely dark. He would stand for a long time at the window, gazing down at the street. In the park across the way black trees, blacker than night, loomed motionless. Beyond them, invisible from the road, was the cemetery with its sparse, feeble street-lamps, of no use to the dead. Nikolai pictured his son's small grave, the ugly grey trapezoid of the gravestone, the cheapest sort, reconstituted from marble dust, the broken-branch ornament painted on in fake gilt... It had all been a long time ago, and he no longer felt anguish at the thought of his son. Besides, he had trained himself never to think of his child's spasms as he held him in his arms. He couldn't even remember for sure when it had happened. Nikolai pressed his forehead to the window, enjoying the sharp sensation of the cold glass against his skin. Yet what still hurt – tormented him unceasingly, endlessly – was that they – no, *he*, the paterfamilias, the father, the husband and man – had not managed a worthy headstone. He had dreamed of a black marble slab with gold lettering, and with that photograph – the most beautiful one, the one Nikolai had most treasured – framed in glass. Nikolai vaguely recalled having set fire to it by accident, or so it seemed to him. He had touched it with a lit match, then watched as it flared gently, the paper burning up unhurriedly, the photograph blazing with strange, wonderful colours in Nikolai's fingers, for a long time numb to the searing pain of the flames.

He heard the door open behind him, then Vera's voice. She had to go to work, to the theatre, and asked if Nikolai would eat dinner with her. He would sometimes agree to these requests, and with an effort tore himself away from the window and stumbled out after her, squinting in the glare. Vera hastened to switch off the light, knowing how it irritated him after the darkness of his room.

Nikolai watched her from his seat at the table as she moved in and out of the kitchen, and knew that Bertrand was right. It's true, Vera is indeed beautiful, infinitely beautiful, he said to himself. She is magnificent, her beauty is so perfect it seems almost otherworldly, almost unreal, ridiculous as it sounds. As though she isn't a real person of flesh and bone and blood, like everyone else – like the neighbours next door, for example, or downstairs. How could it be that this marvellous dream, this figment of the imagination, in spite of everything was living with him in a cramped one-bedroom Khruschevka apartment?

At this point he would start to feel angry at the thought that many others would also find her beautiful, that she must have masses of opportunities to be unfaithful.

Vera left for the theatre early in the morning, and at best came home around eleven – there were endless rehearsals, then performances. She ate her lunch and her dinner there, in the cheap theatre cafeteria, washing down the ubiquitous meat salad with a sour lemonade from a half-litre bottle made of green glass.

So answer me this one simple, one might even say elementary question: who could say exactly what she got up to at her beloved theatre? In the dressing rooms, the bright naked bulbs shine from the mirrors, make-up and face-powder pots are scattered messily across the tables. They put some chairs up against the wall, she lies down on them on her naked back... how can I bear to think of it? Or she sits astride him, and everything is reflected again and again in the smeary triple mirrors.

***

Nikolai demanded repeatedly that she leave the theatre, that she quit her shameless job. Vera would argue and cry, then go away to her mother's for the night. She insisted that her quitting the theatre would leave them with no money, nothing to live on, to buy food like potatoes, black bread, white bread, pasta, meat, eggs, milk, tea, fish, seasonal greens, butter, whatever else it was that they ate...

This was just a trick, an old, tried-and-tested excuse, convenient as the slippers under your bed that you slip into without having to look. If she really wanted to oblige him and quit for good, she could easily find another job. It wasn't as if the theatre paid much. But that was the crux of the problem, of course. *If she wanted to...*

Nikolai knew very well the easiest way for an actress to get a leading role, the quickest way to get noticed. Bertrand called it 'payment in kind'. He laughed as he said it, shamelessly hinting at Vera. He had these disgusting, repugnant eyes when he rolled the words 'in kind' around on his tongue as if they were song lyrics. 'Ah, what a pity I don't happen to be a director at that damned playhouse...'

Again and again Nikolai screamed at her. He hid her clothes so that she couldn't leave the house and go to the theatre. In the end he beat her, too, trying to stay away from her face so as not to tarnish it with bruises. It was hard to say who suffered most from these blows, she or he. Yet things went on as before, morning rehearsals, evening performances...

***

She said that the dressing rooms all had locks, but tell me – does she always lock the door when she has to change before a show? Vera swore that she always, always did, but he didn't believe her: lies, all lies. How could you remember about the door with only ten minutes to go before your entrance, when you're in a hurry, when your heart is racing before the show? Nikolai pictured the actors, with their elegant, almost feminine gestures, their voluptuous, undulating poses – how he hated them – peering through her doorway at her naked flesh, the flesh which was his, belonged to him!

What agony it was, to wait for her return after a performance. Better he had never met her, had never known her, never loved her.

He pictured her before the mirrors, in a blaze of white lights, the door silently opening... The gap between the door and frame grew, and someone watched from the other side, waiting for Vera to acknowledge his presence – of course she knew he was there, knew his desire – before throwing open the door and entering. His hand barely touching the skin, brushing her cheek, then, as they gazed at each other in the triple-panelled mirrors, falling to her shoulder, falling, falling... Nikolai couldn't shake the image of that falling hand, endlessly sliding over Vera's flesh. She closed her eyes, head tilting back, she let herself fall back against her chair as cold lips, so practised at seduction, grazed her skin. Vera's lips trembled, she whispered something, aroused, oh God, just the way she used to whisper to him, the hand still gliding across her body, squeezing her shoulder now, and Vera cried out in sweet agony, her eyes still closed, she moaned almost soundlessly, her nipples hardening beneath the fingers that pressed them, that squeezed her breasts. Now the door was locked, no doubt. Nikolai drank and drank, but the vodka ran out without bringing him peace, while Bertrand sat in the darkened bedroom, watching him, laughing, telling disgusting stories about Vera...

Sometimes Nikolai seriously considered killing her and then himself, thereby ending this torment that seemed to have no escape nor to offer any redemption. My God, he would think, perhaps she would be different if their son was still alive. But their son was dead – go and see for yourselves, you bastards, there in the cemetery – and so she was no longer constrained by his existence, or had to feel ashamed of her behaviour before her child.

NIGHTS

Bertrand walked up behind Nikolai and gave him a heavy pat on the back, to indicate it was time for bed.

'Up we get! Time for beddy-byes! Here, I'll sing you a beautiful lullaby. *Rock-a-bye baby, in the treetop, when the wind blows the cradle will rock. When the bough breaks the cradle will fall...* There – how was that?'

Nikolai lay down and burrowed into the blankets. The room was spinning, but it was even worse when he was slumped at the table, some sharp corner always digging into his face, his legs and back numb. He could barely walk; the room span, the floor lurched. Everything in his room seemed to be falling away from him; it would stay still for a moment, then slide away, stay still, and slide away again and again and again.

He wasn't sleepy. Besides, he needed to know when Vera would be back. Would she return immediately after the show? If not, if she was late, that could mean she had been seeing someone. And God forbid, goddamn it, goddamn it, if that was the case, Nikolai would... He smashed his fists into the wall and felt no pain, even when his hands bled.

***

In the darkness there was a knocking at the door, and Bertrand hurried out into the corridor, while Nikolai, hardly able to raise his head, tried to make out the sliding, spinning green clock-face on the table by the window. She was on time again today. And yesterday, he remembered, yesterday too she was on time. What about the day before that, what had happened the day before that? Did it matter?

He fell back onto the pillow and listened to Bertrand out in the hallway, kissing Vera's fingers. When at last she came into the bedroom, Nikolai lay, eyes closed, facing the wall, trying to breathe evenly, not moving until Vera had fallen asleep.

Once she was sleeping, he turned to face her. He rose silently – worn out, exhausted after her day, she didn't hear him – and turned on the night-light by the window, then returned to the bed, and looked at her face. He did this almost every night, yet strangely it was not enough. He could never satiate his eyes in the way that thirst is quenched with an abundance of water, or hunger sated with food, or bodily fatigue banished by a long sleep... For some reason he couldn't quench his thirst for her beauty, so warm, so dear to him, so perfect as always while she slept; he just couldn't. Maybe Bertrand was right and Nikolai was simply not up to it, talentless, dull, insignificant man that he was? She always grew pale in sleep, her hair falling over her white face, her bloodless lips barely visible in the darkness. Her breath came shallowly, and she would sometimes shudder at something terrible in her dreams. At those moments he longed to take her in his arms, crush her to him, console her and say *I'm here, you have nothing to fear with me by your side, nothing – I would die before I let anyone harm you*. She would whisper in her sleep, then sigh and turn her back on him, and then he had to wait, sometimes for hours, for her to come back to him, so pale and slim, his sleeping darling, his own, his very own, his beautiful, sweet, sleeping beloved. He didn't kiss her, not wanting to wake her by mistake, but sat motionless on the chair by her bedside. Sometimes he fell asleep himself, but always he awoke before she did, so she would never catch him sitting by the bed watching over her, secretly and therefore shamefully, like a criminal drinking in her beauty, which was holy to him as everything about this woman was holy to him. This rare and beautiful woman who by some accident of fate, some providential conjunction of the stars, had come into his life, had become his wife. Had borne him a son. And buried him soon after, never once reproaching him, Nikolai, for the poor child's death. Yet who else was to blame, if not he? He was virtually a murderer – why then had she not accused him?

THE TREES OUTSIDE THE WINDOW

'It stands to reason that a woman can get everything she wants much more easily than a man can,' said Sergeant Bertrand, nodding meaningfully, and Nikolai believed him because it was impossible not to believe him, since he was always right, this Bertrand. 'A man has to be clever, capable, bold... but a woman doesn't need much. You know, when a young girl comes into my office with a tender bosom like your...' Bertrand smiled and rubbed his hands in his habitual manner. 'Well, I give her whatever she wants, don't I? After she's given me what I want, naturally. It's the same thing with your lady wife. What was that role she had in that, you know, that play? Damn, I've completely forgotten. Never mind. It's not important. Anyway, so at first there were three hopefuls, each one desperate to get the part... what was it now? Each candidate lovely as a spring flower, each fresh and slim and fragrant. To say nothing of the... ahem... vital statistics. You get what I'm saying.'

'It was Ophelia, God damn you.'

'At any rate, I was in no hurry. I wanted to have a good look first. The truth is, I liked your wife best straight away, your Verochka. She was head and shoulders above the rest, but there's a kind of process with these things, you know? It's amusing to string it out, to tease them a bit, and tease yourself a bit, too. I knew how it was all going to end, you see, it was hardly my first time. So. We rehearsed the three Ophelias together and – here's the fun part – your wife was by no means given any precedence. On the contrary, she'd been told that she was only included out of courtesy, because we all liked her personally, on the off chance that some latent talent would suddenly evince itself. No, we made out that another girl was the favourite, even though she was nowhere near as good.

'Oh, how she suffered, your Verochka. What a pleasure it was to put her through the wringer, to watch her as someone else pranced about on stage while she sat in the darkened stalls watching and listening, in agonies of envy. Do you have any idea how all-consuming the envy of an actor is? During those weeks Verochka grew thin and pallid, but she looked all the better for it. Do you remember that time? How thin she got?

'And then I asked her to come and see me in my office. If I'm not mistaken, that was the end of the fourth week of rehearsals. There was a performance that night, and everyone had gone home for the afternoon, except for the stage-hands setting up props. I asked Verochka to stay behind and come see me in my office. I'd sent my secretary home, as I always did in such cases.'

***

Vera knew perfectly well why he had asked to see her. He found her in the darkened stalls, passing the time by watching the stage-hands go about their business. He greeted her by kissing her hand in that gallant, slightly old-fashioned way of his. Then, with a furtive glance around, he spoke quietly into her ear so that no one else could hear. If he had needed anything else, if it had been some ordinary work-related matter, he would have spoken in his normal voice: 'My dear, would you mind popping up to my office after rehearsals, it won't take a minute.' Or he would have had the talk right then and there, no need to go to upstairs at all.

She stood by the mirror, bending slightly at her slim waist, touched a tortoiseshell comb to her hair, then tucked it away in her purse. *I've dreamed of playing this part all my life*, she thought. *It could make me famous. Certainly I will be better than anyone else. It's for the sake of art that I am doing this*. She pushed open the heavy black door.

He was already walking towards her, smiling. He kissed her hand, then began to kiss her fingers. Vera felt how sticky his lips were, moist and sticky. Why were they sticky? She shuddered involuntarily, but thankfully he didn't seem to notice. She suddenly felt sad. Very sad, the kind of sadness you feel when a person dear and precious to you unexpectedly dies. In truth she felt not just sad but also empty and depressed and alone, even a little frightened. But not for long. She distracted herself from these unpleasant and superfluous feelings by turning her mind to other things, to the chairs neatly arranged around the table, for example, the trees outside the window, the new sofa which had been lugged inside by four workmen just a few days ago, the trees outside the window, trees outside the window, those trees outside that window... and anyway, why not, what's the difference if no one will ever know? Lie back, girl, and enjoy yourself.

He went to lock the door behind her, then started on her fingers once again, looking up into her face. She looked back at him. She looked at him, and at the window; she could see huge old poplars, silver poplars they were called, calmly swaying in the breeze.

This went on and on, so long that she could no longer bear it. She walked over to the black leather sofa, sat down and, looking straight into the man's eyes, pulled her blouse over her head.

Then she turned her gaze to the window, leant back against the sofa, the ice-cold touch of the black leather sending a brief shudder down her spine.

There was a bad smell about him.

***

Nikolai could see all this because he was sitting in a cabinet or a safe, looking out through some kind of one-way glass or secret mirror, but the doors were locked and he couldn't get out. He screamed and beat at the door, the glass steaming up with his breath, but they – the pair of them in the room – didn't hear him, or didn't want to hear him, or pretended not to hear him.

He saw Bertrand move close to Vera, his hand settling on her breast. He saw her shut her eyes when Bertrand knelt before her, pressing himself against her legs, how she tried briefly to push him away when he began to slide his hands up her skirt, to part her legs, squeezing her knees; how then Vera shut her eyes again and let her hands fall on Bertrand's head as he burrowed his face where her thighs were so pale and tender, unused to sunlight, and was nibbling at them, kissing them, while she lay back on the sofa... Nikolai screamed and screamed, he couldn't bear it, he would go mad, his heart would burst with the pain of it, but they didn't hear him, they kept going, going, going.

***

Nikolai shouted and cried in his sleep, without waking up. Vera sat with him in the darkness, holding his hand, stroking it, wiping his tears, changing the damp cloth on his forehead for another when it grew hot.

***

'And that is precisely why I love this girl, your tender little Verochka,' said Bertrand as he approached the safe inside which Nikolai was thrashing about. 'It's a question of breeding, you see. Breeding is of great importance. Some women will lie down beneath you as if they're begging for alms, but not your Verochka... Oh no, she's the very embodiment of pride and passion. She's using you, not the other way around.'

Bertrand took his time tucking in his shirt and zipping up. He jangled a bunch of keys, looking for the right one, inserted it at last in the keyhole, and turned. The heavy door of the steel cabinet swung open with a creak.

Vera stood motionless by the window, naked, slender arms across her chest. She was leaning slightly backwards, her belly pushed out a little so that it grazed the marble windowsill. She looked out indifferently. Nikolai picked up a carafe from the table and crept towards her. She stood motionless, paying no attention to him, gazing out of window. As he lifted the carafe over his head, ready to strike, the stopper slipped out, and Nikolai was suddenly drenched in a torrent of icy water. Vera turned, as if she had just woken up, only just noticed his presence. She screamed and ran out, down the corridors, still naked, and everyone stopped and looked at her, feasting their eyes on her body.

***

By the time the ambulance arrived, Nikolai was starting to regain his senses. The doctor took his blood pressure, gave him an injection of some kind, murmured something to his wife, who shook her head. He jotted something down in his papers and talked to Nikolai for a long time, his moving lips producing unintelligible sounds as he stood menacingly over Nikolai's bed like some bandit from a picture book.

After the injection Nikolai drifted off to sleep again, lying with his eyes open, while his wife and the tall, grey old man in a white coat, a useless stethoscope around his neck, stood over him. The old man was talking loudly, almost shouting. For some reason he seemed angry with Nikolai's wife, as though she were refusing something.

Then everything went black, the sounds vanished, and out of the darkness a terrifying ball of fire floated into view.

LONG DREAMS

The next time Bertrand came later than usual, when it was already dark. They lit up and sat together in silence for a long while. Eventually Bertrand rose and put out his cigarette in the ashtray. He went to the window and drew back the curtains: the room seemed to grow a little lighter.

'You're looking especially glum today,' said Bertrand, smirking as he sat himself down again in the armchair. Nikolai could hear him extruding another cigarette from the pack, rolling and working it in his fingers before he put it on the table in front of him.

'There's just one thing I want to remember,' Nikolai said. 'You know, after this – he pointed at the scar on his forehead – well, after this happened, I forgot things, everything got jumbled together and I can't remember anything. Whether I dreamed a thing or if it really happened, or if it's something I heard about. I sometimes have to ask Vera which it is. It's ridiculous.'

He fell silent.

'What exactly are you trying to remember?' said Bertrand, picking up the cigarette again and lighting it.

'No, it was a dream, it must have been... Such things only happen in dreams. I dreamed I was a child. I was seven or eight, in the dream, maybe nine. It's strange, the dream was so very long.' Nikolai smiled. 'Still, dreams can be like that.'

Bertrand nodded, yes, they can...

'Scientists have discovered that dreams actually last only a few moments – just fractions of a second – but afterwards it feels as though you've lived through hours, days, weeks, months, years. That's what happened to me. I remember going fishing in that dream. It used to be a passion of mine. It was what I loved best, going to the river, just me and my fishing rod, on my own. But this wasn't a good dream – I didn't catch anything, not a single fish. Imagine my disappointment. I just got cold, so freezing cold...'

'That's because of the open window,' said Bertrand.

Nikolai looked at him, puzzled. 'What does that have to...?'

'There was an open window in your bedroom. It was cold outside, so you dreamed about being cold.'

'Yes, I suppose... you must be right. Of course... I played football too, in the same dream.'

Nikolai screwed shut his eyes and fiery little figures ran to and fro beneath his eyelids. There was a lengthy silence.

'What was I talking about?' he said at last. 'Oh yes, the dream. I was playing football. But that isn't the main thing, even though I did dream it all in great detail.

I went outside, on my own. I hung around the front yard, by our block of apartments, then climbed up the tree, I think, then down again. We had this tree in the yard, with a thick low-hanging branch, perfect for climbing. I was bored. And hot. It was very hot...'

He was remembering more easily now, though it wasn't exactly remembering. No, the events of his dream were alive before his eyes. It was more like watching a play at the theatre and telling the man in the seat next to his what was happening on the stage. Though in fact the analogy was flawed, since anyone sitting next to him would have had a very good view of the stage himself, and describing the proceedings to him would have been completely pointless. Unless the man in the next seat was blind? Was Bertrand like the blind man in the next seat?

'Anyway, I finally sat down by the entrance to the neighbouring block. There was a bench in the shade. It was cooler there. I saw a cat come out from the basement; it was ginger, I remember. My mother always said ginger cats bring you luck so I decided I would try and catch it. I sat there, keeping as still as I could, anxious not to frighten the cat by a careless move. She came to sit in a sunspot, and very tenderly coiled her tail around herself. She didn't notice me at all. She raised her head and looked up at the sun, and I could see her pupils – you know, these dark, thin, narrow slits? They grew even narrower, contracting until they almost disappeared into her pale cat's eyes. You see, I even remember the colour of her eyes. They were this strange yellow-green that you only ever see on cats.

'I was poised to spring forward and grab her. The cat was very close to me, and I figured I could reach her in a single bound. Very slowly and inconspicuously I tilted forward, planting my feet in readiness for a quick strong leap. The cat, meanwhile, began to lick her paw; she was too busy grooming herself to give me any notice. This was a very dignified, very neat cat, you see. But just as I was on the point of pouncing, somebody slammed a balcony door shut above our heads.'

'And?'

'And... Nothing. It just startled the cat. Finally noticing me, she crouched low to the ground – then something fell from above and landed in the front garden. That gave her a real fright and she legged it back to the basement.'

Nikolai turned to Bertrand. 'My whole life might have been different if I'd caught that cat.'

'Are you serious?' said Bertrand. 'Tell me you're joking.'

'Well, it was ginger. They bring luck. Isn't that what mother said?'

Bertrand burst out laughing.

Nikolai poured out more vodka, drank it down.

'But I didn't mind. I mean, I did mind at the time but it quickly passed, the way sadness passes quickly when you're a child. I looked up: there were men on the first-floor balcony. They were hooting with laughter. There were two of them, and they were looking down into the garden below. One of them was pointing. I figured they had lost something. I was a curious boy and I was dying to know what they had dropped down there. But as well as being curious, I was proud: I couldn't let them see me run over and look. But they wouldn't go inside. So I just sat there on the shady bench, pretending I couldn't care less about their idiotic guffawing, or about whatever it was they had dropped from the balcony. And then...'

For some reason it suddenly seemed to Nikolai that Bertrand had begun to look agitated.

'Then, the front door opened and I saw her.'

For a moment, Nikolai couldn't speak. He had to clear his throat before he could continue.

'Who did you see?'

'Her,' Nikolai repeated irritably. 'A girl. *The* girl.'

'And what was so extraordinary about her?' asked Bertrand. 'About this particular girl.'

'Nothing, I guess.'

'Nothing at all?' Bertrand spoke in the manner of a man who already knew the answer.

'Nothing at all. Except she was naked.'

In the darkness Bertrand chuckled. It was a galling, gratingly familiar sound; it was how Bertrand chuckled when he looked at Nikolai's wife, at Vera.

'Naked? What do you mean, she was naked? I can't believe my ears. You're telling me she really went outside naked? As in, completely unclothed?'

'Yes,' Nikolai said quietly. 'She was completely naked.'

'That's what's called an erotic dream.'

'No, that is not what's called an erotic dream,' said Nikolai furiously. He had an urge to strike Bertrand.

'All right, all right. Don't be cross. That's not what it's called. My goodness! Aren't we touchy today!'

The image slowly came back into view and Nikolai soon forgot Bertrand was still there in the armchair beside him.

'I can't describe what I felt back then. I was still a child, you see. I was nine years old at most, and yet somehow I knew, in a flash. It was as though I'd suddenly grown up. At first I felt terribly frightened, ashamed and frightened, and wrong. I even thought for a moment, I must be crazy. How else could I be seeing her there, naked, in broad daylight? But that was only to start with. Later it passed.'

Bertrand was chuckling softly again, but Nikolai barely noticed.

'She was drunk. It was obvious even to a child. She was dead drunk, she could barely stand. She had to lean against the wall to keep from falling.

'She stumbled towards the garden, then stopped and turned towards me. It took such a long time for her to turn her head! I don't know why it's so hard for me to remember, so painful. She turned her head slowly, slowly, and then she suddenly looked straight at me. I shut my eyes, thinking she would be embarrassed to be seen naked, even by a kid like me, a stupid little boy who didn't know anything yet.

'Then I heard her laughing. I opened my eyes: she was looking at me and laughing. She had big white teeth. For some reason I thought they must be very sharp. Big, white and sharp. I shut my eyes again.'

'As if that would do any good,' Bertrand scoffed.

'Just before I shut my eyes again, I saw her turn away and go back towards the garden. I heard the grass swish as she moved. Even though she was drunk she trod lightly, but I could make out each quiet step until they ceased. Then she stopped. The bushes rustled, there was laughter from above, she said something thickly in reply. I couldn't understand a word. Then I heard her steps again. She was already near the door when she stopped abruptly and came towards me. I wanted to run away. But it was no longer just fear and shame. No, I also wanted to open my eyes.

'The steps fell silent right next to me and I felt her lips on mine. She was kissing me.'

Bertrand let out a bark of laughter and jiggled around in his chair.

'Her lips were soft and tender. No one had ever kissed me that way before. Once, a girl, a school friend, had kissed me on the cheek. But it was completely different. I can't explain to you, now, what it was that I felt. I may have fainted momentarily; my head was completely empty. My lips hurt – perhaps she had bitten me? Then I heard her laugh again, and the pain vanished. I opened my eyes. She went up to the door, opened it, and it slammed shut behind her.

'I ran home immediately. I shut myself in the bathroom and sat there, perhaps for an hour or so. I couldn't think. No, that's not right... I thought about what I'd seen. I recalled her.'

Nikolai fell silent.

'And?'

'I fell in love with her. I was in love with her, that's how I see it now anyway. Back then I probably didn't even know the phrase. I followed her around, hiding near the entrance to her block, waiting for her to come out. I hung around wherever she went. She was still only a schoolgirl, but she had scores of men. At the time, I didn't really understand, of course. It's only now that I realise...

'What did I – just a little kid – actually want from her? I've no idea. I never thought about it. I was simply perishing for love of her. It was mad. And despite everything, she was so pure. She was so astonishingly beautiful.

'I can imagine how they laughed, those freaks, as they watched us from above. Now I can see that they'd got her drunk, stripped her naked and thrown her clothes out. Why? Maybe in some way she enjoyed it too... They were much older than her.'

'What strange dreams you've had, my boy,' said Bertrand. He was already lighting up again.

'Yes... And there was another evening... Or it was night, really, and I was mooching around by her block as usual, hoping she would come out. It had been dark for a while, and it was time for me to go home, and I was just about to... when she emerged. Of course she wasn't alone. She never seemed to leave the apartment just on her own. At first they walked side by side, but as they passed the building he embraced her. She was laughing. I could barely see in the dark, but I followed the sound of her laughter. They walked around for ages, and I followed. They ended up in the park. There was an alley there, right by the fence, where there were no street-lights, where it was dark.

'They sat down. She never stopped laughing. He talked and she laughed. I could picture her white teeth.

'I hid myself in the bushes, very near. They had no idea I was there, of course, and I could only just make them out, very vaguely – it was night and there were no street-lamps. Soon he began to unbutton her blouse. And the girl just kept laughing.

'She was really still just a girl, no more than sixteen: she was supposed to graduate from school that summer. But to me she seemed so grown-up, a mature woman...'

He looked at Bertrand. Nikolai couldn't make out his face now, only a dark silhouette against the window. The glowing orange disc of his cigarette illuminated his fingertips.

Nikolai was silent for a long time before he again started talking.

'I thought I could see him kissing her legs. I felt terrible. I'd never seen such things before. It was repulsive. I kept thinking I would get up, walk up to them, and kill the bastard. It seemed to me that the things he was doing were a dreadful insult to... I don't know... to her purity, her beauty. An affront to all that made her so lovely, so feminine, so vulnerable. I didn't know how I was going to kill him and I didn't care. I would just walk up and kill him. Strangle him. Yes, strangle him with my bare hands. I was no match for him, of course, he could have seen me off with one hand tied behind his back, but I didn't think of that. In that state I probably was capable of killing him.

'I was crying, and the tears made it even harder to see. They clouded my vision. I tore off some leaves and stuffed them in my mouth – to keep from making a noise, I suppose.

'Then she began to scream. I didn't realise it was her, at first. I strained to see better, I crawled forward a bit, even though I was frightened. Frightened to death now. I still couldn't believe that the screams were coming from her; she was squealing now – and then howling, an inhuman, animal howl of savage pain and terror. I forced myself to creep closer, out from my hiding place, though my hands were numb with fear. I was only a few steps away from the bench. She started choking, like someone was pouring water into her mouth, drowning her. I...'

Nikolai picked up the glass. Finding it empty, he groped in the darkness for the bottle and poured another measure. He didn't notice how much his hands were shaking.

'Did you see anything?'

'I can't remember. Something, maybe...'

Nikolai shut his eyes, trying to remember.

'No. No. I fainted. For real this time, not metaphorically. I fainted from sheer terror. Maybe I saw something, but I can't remember. The hideous way she screamed. I never heard a human being scream like that.

'When I finally came to, it was quiet. Unnaturally silent. I could hear the blood rushing around inside my skull. I lay still for ages, afraid to move, afraid someone would see me and drag me out. I crawled backwards, deeper into the bushes, lay there for a while listening, and when I was sure there was no one around and no one was after me, I ran home. God, how I ran, how I ran... I had probably never run so fast in my life, with such desperation.

'When I got home, I was unable to speak, but no one noticed. I was told to get straight into the bath; I was plastered with mud – my trousers, my shirt, my hands, my face. In the bath I started to calm down a bit. Strangely, I fell asleep almost immediately afterwards. That happens. The worst was to come. At school the next day kids were saying that someone had been murdered in the park the night before. The park was right behind the school, you could see it from all the back windows. I'll never forget the animated, happy faces of the girls as they relayed this news to me. What a thing to happen, and right by the school too! No one could talk about anything else that day. Students or teachers. The conduct of the murdered girl, our class teacher told us confidentially, had not been irreproachable. You could say she had brought it on herself. Such a thing could never have happened to a decent girl. It was inconceivable. I won't say there was no pity for her at all. Of course there was. Of course everyone pitied her, especially the male staff, who could not have been blind to her astonishing beauty, not to mention her availability. Yes, they all pitied her – but more than they pitied her, they judged her. Not even that, they simply understood why this should happen to her of all people, only to her and to no one else. And they thought that was how it should be.

'She was too beautiful and free. Young, beautiful and free. Her beauty was too vivid, like a challenge. Everyone knows: too much of anything is no good to anyone, beauty included. And she had too much beauty. Naturally it drove them mad, the old bags. Who wouldn't be driven mad?

'All the time I was terrified the police would find out I'd been in the park that night... I almost forgot to say – before lessons began a few of the bolder boys, myself included, had raced over there to *have a look*. The dead have a mysterious power over children. I was frightened. I didn't want to go there with the others and yet I was irresistibly drawn back. There were rumours that she had been murdered with extraordinary cruelty, with a savagery that defied explanation, that she had been diabolically tortured. That she hadn't been murdered so much as tortured to death, a slow, protracted death.

'The place was ringed with police and obviously they didn't let anyone get near. But we crawled through the bushes and nobody noticed us. I don't know how but we ended up exactly where I had lain the night before.'

Nikolai covered his face with his hands.

'She was lying on the ground, one leg for some reason resting on the bench. She was completely naked and incredibly pale, as though there wasn't a drop of blood left in her. Her belly was red, though. It looked like it had been torn open – not cut, but actually torn open... I couldn't quite see because they came and covered her with something, some kind of cloth.

'I don't remember how I got back to school... They did find the killer. It was very easy. He didn't even try to hide. The sniffer dog led them straight to his apartment. They rang the bell, but there was no answer. Then they broke down the door and went in – and there he was, hanging from a noose.

'That night, when he took her to the park, it was too dark for me to get a good look at him. But he was young, still just a lad, only a bit older than her. Tall, a bit weedy. Longish hair. That was all I had time to see.'

Nikolai paused.

'And that's my dream.'

'After a dream like that you might never wake up,' said Bertrand sharply. He took a drag; the light fell on his face and Nikolai shuddered at the sight of it.

'What's the matter?' Bertrand smiled, but Nikolai could no longer see his face. The cigarette had been lowered into the ashtray.

'It just gave me a fright, that's all. It was so dark – and then a light, out of nowhere.'

After a time, Nikolai said: 'I thought...'

'What did you think?'

'When you took that drag... Your face lit up from below. When I was a boy, we used to try and creep each other out that way, shining a light just beneath. I thought for a moment you didn't have any eyes. You had holes for eyes. And no skin on your face.'

'What a fevered, gloomy imagination you have, my precious lad,' Bertrand said drily from the darkness.

THEATRE

Nikolai was in two minds whether to tell his wife he was going to see her perform at the theatre. In the end he decided against. Better to see Vera just as others saw her every day. Better she didn't know about it.

As soon as she had left that evening, he put on the only suit he owned, with a clean white shirt and a tie. He had lost weight and the suit, unworn for several years, was too big. There was a half-empty bottle on the round table in the living room. Nikolai half-filled a glass, drank. The vodka seemed weak and flat. Without bothering to get anything to eat, he emptied the bottle. He started to feel a little queasy. At the door he pulled the tie over his head and threw it onto the floor. He was no longer used to wearing one and it made him feel awkward and constrained. The thing was too tight around his neck and stopped him from breathing freely.

Nikolai walked through the silent park, not looking at the few passers-by. He took deep breaths of the sharp, frosty air. The dense clusters of black trees made it darker still. Emerging into the road, he flagged a taxi and soon arrived at the brightly-lit theatre. He bought a ticket in the stalls and left his coat at the cloakroom.

Ignoring the queue, he walked straight to the bar, bought a glass of champagne and downed it in one. The bottle had just been uncorked and the strong fizz made him gag. He was extremely nervous.

The play was about to begin, but there were still a lot of people in the corridors, chatting, looking at the posters and photos hanging on the walls, looking at each other, looking at him, Nikolai. They seemed to be staring at him with particular interest, as though they knew that he was *her* husband, the spouse of that astonishing woman who would appear on stage later. The unremarkable, grey, insignificant man and the dazzling beauty who bewitched everyone. They were smiling, and Nikolai knew it was because of the cartoonish contrast between husband and wife. Not to mention their sympathy for the wife: such a beauty with such a dull husband!

High on the wall, next to the ceiling, was a row of actors' photographs, their names and initials on the frames. Nikolai walked along them, head tilted back, carefully studying the faces, and was noted with satisfaction that most of them were not nearly as attractive as one might have expected. That went for the women too. But then he froze, thunderstruck: there was a photograph of his own wife, and next to it, one of the director. Anyone could see at a glance the bond that existed between them! The man was smiling, his gaze directed at Vera's photograph. It was an impudent, sleazy smile. He was looking at her as though awaiting her reaction to some filthy double-entendre. Or he'd just made a sordid proposition and was now expecting her response, turning towards her, certain that she would acquiesce.

'What a beauty!' A voice behind him startled Nikolai.

He turned to see an old man. Once he had Nikolai's attention he gave an exaggerated sigh, rubbed his bald spot and gestured towards the wall as if to say, shame I didn't meet a girl like that when I was young, I would have known what to do with her, I can tell you! Plucking a little pink hanky from his inner pocket, he blew his nose with a horrid grimace.

Afraid that he would strike the old man down, Nikolai turned and almost ran into the auditorium.

THE OLD MAN WITH BINOCULARS

The huge chandelier slowly dimmed. All around people rustled their programs, raising them to their eyes to try to read them in the darkness. Strange to say, the same old man took the seat on Nikolai's right. He blew his nose again.

The curtain opened and people Nikolai had never seen before began to move around the stage. He had no idea what it was about and didn't even try to follow as he waited anxiously for his wife's entrance. The old man began to polish a pair opera glasses with his handkerchief. They gleamed dimly in the darkness.

From time to time a line of dialogue made its way into Nikolai's consciousness. He was amazed at the complete idiocy of every single one.

***

'Is it really you?'

'Yes.'

'How wonderful.'

'How could you think I would be tempted?'

'When you're in love, you don't think rationally.'

'Two hearts aflame for one another – that's what love is!'

She struck a pretty pose, one foot extended coyly. He slowly walked to the window, behind which a round, badly stuck-on, creased-looking golden moon shone against a painted sky.

'A shovel lay across his breast...'

'No, it cannot be! You must tell me the whole truth!'

'I shall! I shall tell you, but not until tomorrow, after the sun has risen!'

Before the audience's eyes, the window floated slowly upwards and a heavy set of office furniture came down from somewhere near the ceiling, rocking and shuddering as it descended.

New people... more stilted dialogue... jerky movements...

'That's exactly what they told him at the meeting – "no"! Can you imagine?'

'You must be joking – it's not possible!'

'Not only is it possible, I'm telling you it actually happened. I saw it with my own ears.'

***

This last line was spoken by a young actor, almost a child. He must have just started at the theatre. Nikolai saw an livid blush spread over his face as he looked out at the audience. Stammering, he fell silent, eyes bulging in dumb panic.

Nikolai burst out laughing, slapping his knees and filling the auditorium with the sound of his guffaws. He didn't even hear the boy on the stage hurriedly mumble his way through the rest of his lines.

***

When the intermission came, she still hadn't appeared on stage. Nikolai followed the old man out, purchased a programme from a woman in a blue staff uniform, and located Vera's name among the cast list. Then they went over to the bar where, again ignoring the queue, he ordered two coffees and a glass of champagne.

They sat at a table in a dark corner of the room. The old man savoured his coffee, taking small lip-smacking sips. Once he had finished, he began to speak. Nikolai wasn't really listening. He fiddled with his glass and furtively scanned the room, not wanting to meet anyone he knew. Meanwhile the old man took out his handkerchief, grimaced, blew his nose, for some reason peered into his empty cup, waved his arms about and stroked his bald spot – talking the whole time, incessantly talking without pausing for breath.

'Come on.' Nikolai rose and straightened his coat. 'That was the bell.'

They returned to their seats.

***

The kid who had messed up his lines was now sauntering around the stage in a dandyish, glued-on goatee and moustache. From time to time he stroked his freshly-acquired pot-belly in an effort to portray a grown-up, serious, important personage.

He seemed to be playing some sort of boss. This consisted of punching switchboard buttons and talking into the speaker-phone in a harsh, false voice. One moment he was tearing into some unseen person with much banging on the desk and reddening of the face. The next he was signing orders with pitiless abandon, shaking his head whenever asked for anything. All the while he was sweating horrifically, so that damp stains bloomed instantly where his shirt came into contact with his torso.

***

All the signs were that he was the boss of some important institution. In the office stood an enormous safe, into which from time to time he shoved some papers. Occupying centre stage was a conference table with a multitude of chairs around it. The walls were panelled with varnished wood, and to the right was a black sofa with carved wooden armrests. Everyone who entered this office immediately assumed a pathetic and bewildered demeanour, speaking in obsequious tones, all but bowing and scraping.

The boss was seated and, brow furrowed, was writing rapidly. His pen moved theatrically over a piece of paper. There was a knock at the door and – a touch more swiftly than he would have done so in real life – he raised his head.

'Come in!' he barked, then smiled as the door opened.

Somewhere below his heart, deep in his chest, something clenched painfully inside Nikolai and everything went black. *It was his wife!*

The boss rose slowly and walked up to her, neatly arranging the chairs around the table. He motioned her to a seat. White-faced, she didn't meet his eyes.

'What's this about?' He went to the door and shut it firmly.

'I... I came to say I can't oblige you.'

'Well, in that case I am forced to conclude that you don't really love your husband,' he replied, looking brazenly into her face.

'That's not for you to say. I love my husband deeply,' she said emphatically.

'I'm afraid that simply cannot be true. Or perhaps you haven't understood the precarious circumstances he finds himself in. He will perish...'

The old man elbowed him sharply. Nikolai turned to look at him: he was frenetically polishing the lenses of his opera glasses with his handkerchief.

Nikolai shut his eyes, sat for a few moments, then re-focused on the stage. His palms were sweating and he rubbed them on his trousers.

'I am quite serious. Your husband is completely in my power.'

'You are a scoundrel,' said Vera quietly.

'That's beside the point, my dear. I can do with him as I like.'

'But you were friends once! Don't you remember...'

She was close to tears.

'Why dredge up the past?' he said, laughing. Then with a swift, sudden movement he fell to his knees and pressed his lips to her hand.

'How can you be so blind? Don't you know I would do anything for you?' he went on quickly, kissing her fingers. 'I'd give you anything you asked for! My dearest, my darling, you need only say the word! How I adore you! I'm yours, all yours, just say the word...'

Nikolai jumped up from his chair, then sank back into it. Breathless, he clawed at the top button of his shirt, but it was no use. His fingers refused to work. Blood pounded thickly and heavily at his temples.

'My God,' said Vera. 'How I hate you.'

'As you like, but the main thing is that I adore you. You need only say the word and I'll arrange everything!'

The old man gave him another prod with elbow. He was glued to his opera glasses, his whole body leaning forward. His sharp elbow dug beneath Nikolai's ribs, but he didn't register the pain.

After a long silence his wife said, 'Save him.'

The kneeling man stood up and brushed his fingers across her cheek.

'Save him...'

Nikolai saw that the old man's knee was jiggling.

The woman, looking into the man's eyes, walked over to the sofa and sat down. Turning towards the man, who hadn't moved, she sighed and with a single movement pulled her blouse over her head.

The crowd gasped for breath.

The old man, eyes riveted to the stage, muttered feverishly to himself: 'bosoms, bosoms, bosoms...'

Nikolai vision went dark again; a black spot loomed before his eyes. But then the blackness vanished and again he could see the stage.

The man came towards Vera slowly, gawping, ogling her pure, shining white breasts. Then he suddenly fell on her, toppling her backwards onto the sofa, and the curtain began to drop. The old man shot to his feet and applauded wildly, clapping his wizened little hands together, opera glasses tucked prissily under one arm. He turned excitedly to Nikolai.

'Those bosoms, did you see them? A goddess!'

Nikolai rose unsteadily, took a swing, and with all his might struck the old man in the face with the back of his hand. Without looking back, not hearing the old man's shrieks behind him, he ran for the exit.

EVENING

Nikolai paced outside for a long time, not feeling the cold though his coat was unbuttoned. He lit up again and again, but then flicked each cigarette into the snow without smoking it to the end. He saw the white ambulance arrive; he saw the doctor emerge, closing the door behind him with a slam that resounded in the still air; from his place behind a row of young pine trees, he saw them leading out the old man by the arms, pressing something white to his face. He heard the old man shouting, in a thin and breaking voice: 'He's insane! I did nothing! I don't know what happened. He's a lunatic, he ought to be apprehended... He had blonde hair, make a note of that. And a scar on his forehead. Make a note!'

He continued from inside the ambulance: 'It hurts, oh, it hurts! Please! Give me something for the pain!'

The car sped off and it was quiet again. Nikolai buttoned up, not because he was cold – he didn't even notice the cold – but purely out of habit. And so when he wanted another smoke he had to unbutton again, to extricate the pack of cigarettes and the matches from his jacket.

He had a tormenting sense that what had just happened to him inside the theatre had already happened, that he had lived through it once already. It was such a strong feeling, as though the memory was just about to come back to him... all he had to do was focus... He kneaded his scalp, pressing his temples, to get the thick, coagulated blood in his veins flowing – but when he shut his eyes all he could see were leaping fiery figures.

He couldn't understand how he had ended up outside. He had wanted to run to the stage, and yet instead he had hurried the other way, to the exit, down the deserted unlit hallways. He had thrown his token down in front of the woman at the cloakroom – for some reason she had given him a frightened look – and while she ran to fetch his things he had stood there groaning, gritting his teeth through the pain, head swaying from side to side.

There was one act to come – the third, the last – and then they'd all go home, Nikolai thought. The audience and the actors. And her too. Nikolai turned up his collar to cover his face and backed further into the shadow of the trees, away from the bright street-lights at the entrance. He would wait. He had nowhere to rush off to.

***

Vera ran past him on the path, hurrying to catch a bus. Nikolai recognised her from behind. The doors closed immediately after she'd climbed on and the bus pulled away from the stop. Nikolai went back to the theatre.

When he saw the actors leaving via the stage door he walked over.

He recognised *that* actor straight away. He was on his own. He put on a fur hat, then paused, looked around, delved into his pocket and began to fiddle with a pair of gloves, slowly and meticulously encasing one finger at a time. Nikolai walked up to him, holding out his ticket.

'Excuse me?' he said as he approached.

'Yes?' The actor gave him a friendly look.

'Might I have your autograph?'

Flattered, the man smiled.

'But of course. It would be my pleasure.'

Here, outside, he no longer seemed quite so young or uncertain, and he now had a rich, sonorous voice. Producing a tiny pencil, he made a rapid mark.

'Thank you, thank you so much. Just one more thing, though...'

'Oh... yes?' The actor turned towards him absent-mindedly.

'It's a delicate matter... could we go just over there?' Nikolai pointed to the pines.

The actor was silent.

'You know what, why don't you piss off,' he said finally, and made to step around Nikolai, who grabbed him by the arm and gave a violent tug, dragging him behind the trees.

The man tried to throw the first punch, but Nikolai blocked him, then punched him twice beneath the jaw, then in the stomach, then in the face again, and hearing it crunch, knew that he'd smashed the man's teeth in.

The actor managed somehow to stay upright, staring inanely at Nikolai. His fur hat lay in the snow, large gobbets of blood fell from his chin, onto his coat and the snow at his feet.

Nikolai stepped back, and kicked – the actor tumbled backwards and smacked his head on a tree trunk. For a long time Nikolai kicked him, then he bent over to punch aiming precisely at his head and throat, using all the force he could muster, until the man in the snow stopped moving.

When he had finished Nikolai hastily wiped his feverish face and hands with snow and, avoiding the road, walked through the deep snow to the bus stop.

***

Vera went to her mother's. But she was back in a week. By then the bruises on her body had faded, or else she had cleverly camouflaged them with make-up. Only the base of her throat was still blotched yellow and blue.

Vera wept and pleaded for forgiveness. Nikolai made her swear never to return to the theatre. Never on any account. He made her swear on the memory of their son. Unbeknownst to him, Vera had begged the actor not to go to the police and he had obliged. She took on a temporary job as a yard-sweeper while her mother and friends tried to find her other work.

CHURCH

When Nikolai woke up in the morning, he couldn't drag himself out of bed for a long time. His body felt weak; his head was heavy; he just didn't have the strength to get up. He lay there for another hour, drifting in and out of fitful sleep. But he knew he had to get up. He tossed back the covers, sat up abruptly and nearly toppled back again. The sudden movement had made his head spin. After a while he managed to swing his legs to the floor, feeling for his slippers.

Vera would have left breakfast out for him before she went to work, as she always did. But he didn't feel like going to the kitchen. Instead he walked to the table, picked up a bit of yesterday's stale bread left on a saucer and chewed it with an effort. The vodka was all gone. Yesterday he'd broken open the last bottle from the stash he hid away from himself in the cupboard. Forcing down a mouthful of tasteless bread, Nikolai picked up a glass and downed the last dregs of vodka – or maybe it was water, he couldn't tell. Then he began to get dressed.

***

The whole way, Nikolai thought about how there wasn't any vodka left and how he would have to queue again, jostle his way into the spirits section, sequestered from the rest of the store by steel bars. He could go and knock on the back door, of course, and skip the queue by paying over the odds, but money was scarce, as always. His veteran's pension was usually gone in the first week, and the greater part of his wife's salary soon after that. No, it wasn't his style to skip the queue. Leave that to the capitalists. He wasn't proud. He could stand and wait like everybody else. We're humble folk, all we ask for is our pension. We may not be rich, but we are deserving. The government is paying us damages for injuries we sustained, to compensate us for our war wounds, for the blood we poured like fertilizer onto the Afghan soil.

Nikolai laughed bitterly and spat into the snow.

The church wasn't far, ten minutes or so to walk. Nikolai wasn't sure why he was going. He had no idea what he was going to say or what he was hoping to hear in reply. It was simply that the night before he had decided, before falling asleep, he would go; that's all he remembered.

Soon he was in the church. The service was long over and it was nearly empty.

Not knowing what to do with himself, Nikolai walked up and down, looking abstractedly around him. He was aware of the icons with their golden vestments, the guttering candles, but he felt indifferent. He breathed in the strange, sweet, slightly discomfiting scent.

With a spasm of irritation he realised how ridiculous he must look. He was walking around with his head raised, goggling at the childish pictures, like he was waiting for... what? Why had he come here? He couldn't give a coherent answer.

There was a kind of rustling whisper to his right, and he turned to look. In a dim corner by the door stood a clutch of old women, all dressed in black. Even though they weren't looking at Nikolai, he was sure they were whispering about him.

How much more stupid would he seem if he were to approach to the priest? He, a grown man with all his faculties intact, asking for aid and advice from a complete stranger! How could this man possibly give a damn for Nikolai's troubles and misfortunes? No doubt he would forget all about Nikolai's story the second he was out the door!

Nikolai cursed under his breath. No, he was a fool, a complete idiot for coming here. Why in the world had he come to the church? What had prompted him to drag himself to this place? Did he want to unburden his soul? Was that it? Nikolai groaned with rage and shame at his own weakness.

'Are you all right?' came a voice behind him. Nikolai reared back, startled.

'What?'

A woman of middle age and middling height stood before him. Her head was covered in an old faded kerchief and she wore an equally faded dark housecoat. Her eyes looked moist, as though she had just been crying.

'Are you unwell?' she asked and the concern in her voice only enraged him all the more. Stupid bitch with her fake humility, he thought with revulsion. Compassion as duty.

'I'm fine,' he said. 'I'm just fine and dandy.'

The woman – frightened, it seemed to Nikolai – placed a finger to her lips.

'Shh. You mustn't speak so loudly in the temple.'

'Oh, it's a temple? And there was me thinking it was just a church.' He thrust his hands into his pockets. 'So how do people speak in here? Is it against the rules to say anything in a human way? To talk like normal, healthy people do?'

The woman knitted her brows and her entire face took on a determined expression, as though she was getting ready for a fight with Nikolai. He was amused.

'It is customary to speak quietly while inside a temple,' the woman told him firmly. 'What's more, I'm not deaf and can hear you perfectly well. Now, what was it you wanted?'

'Me? I...' Nikolai had to stop and think. He glanced from side to side. 'I need a... the person who... The minister. Or whatever you call it.'

For a moment, she looked taken aback, the look he had earlier taken as fear.

'You mean the reverend father? The priest? You've come a bit too late, pretty much everyone has gone. There's only Father Vladimir, he's in the chancel, but he's about to go too... What is it you need?'

That was the question he had dreaded.

'To talk to him,' Nikolai said shortly.

'I think he's about to emerge from the sanctuary, but I doubt he'll have time for you now, he's very busy. He's half an hour late already...'

She broke off in mid-sentence, reacting to some movement behind Nikolai.

'Here he comes,' she whispered. 'Just be quick and get straight to the heart of the matter.'

Nikolai turned around. A tall, slim man was approaching him, buttoning up a plain and thin grey coat over his simple black cassock as he walked. His face was stern and severe. To Nikolai he seemed very pale and somehow depleted.

'Is that your Father Vladimir, then?' He had unconsciously dropped his voice, but the woman was no longer at his side.

Nikolai turned again towards the priest. 'The heart of the matter,' he said to himself in exasperation, remembering the woman's words, 'the heart of the matter...' But what exactly was it supposed to mean, 'the heart of the matter'? How was he meant to know what it was? He wasn't even sure he wanted to go near the man, never mind tell him anything!

The priest drew alongside him. In a moment he would have passed him by without a glance, but Nikolai, despite himself, reached out and plucked at the man's sleeve. His head was buzzing feverishly.

'Just a moment.' Nikolai moistened his lips, which had suddenly gone dry. 'I want to tell you something. I want to talk.'

The priest halted and turned his stern face to Nikolai. 'I'm listening.'

'I wanted to say that I am suffering greatly. I am in pain, it's killing me. I just don't know what to do.'

The priest looked calmly at Nikolai. 'What has happened?'

'I don't know how to explain it...' Nikolai struggled to form the right words. 'It's my wife... I don't know how I can live with my wife anymore.'

He had a strange sense that here in church, talking to a priest, ordinary words would not be enough, he had to find a special, more meaningful set of words to explain himself.

'My wife is bad. Very bad.' He felt the heat rising in his face.

'So make her good,' the priest replied and suddenly smiled. It was a kind and gentle smile that looked out of place on that stern visage.

'You don't understand! She is very, very bad!' Nikolai grew agitated. He hadn't made himself understood. 'She tortures me! She mocks me, and lies to me! There's nothing she won't stoop to, there's nothing sacred for her! All she thinks about is her own...'

He could no longer talk. The emotion was suffocating him.

'Hear the words of the Church's great teacher, St John Chrysostom,' said the priest. 'Though your wife has greatly sinned against you, forgive her all her trespasses; if you have taken to wife a woman of bad temper, teach her to be kind and meek; if she has a failing, drive out the failing and not your wife. If after many trials you believe your wife to be incorrigible and unwilling to give up her bad habits, even then do not cast her aside, for she is flesh of your flesh, as it is said: two become one. Though her failings be ineradicable, you shall have great reward that you continue to instruct and reason with her.'

Nikolai cut him off. 'You're not listening to me, damn you! How can I make you see? What you've just said to me, it's all true, it all sounds great, all these beautiful inspiring words of wisdom – but they have nothing to do with what's happening to me! It isn't right, it isn't fair for her to just carry on tormenting me! Why should I be made to suffer? Why must she torment me? Aren't you on the side of justice here? What have I ever done to her, to deserve this? Have I ever wronged her?'

'Ask yourself,' the priest said quietly, 'whether you have not done harm to some other woman in the past, and whether the wound you gave her is being healed now through another woman, your own wife making you atone for the harm you did to another, as a surgeon excises an ulcer. The Holy Scripture tells us that a bad wife is given unto a sinner as punishment. Let a cruel wife be given unto a sinful husband, that she should be as a drawer-out of the poisons that ail him.'

'What are you talking about?' Nikolai was breathless with anger and hurt. 'So it's all my fault? It's all on me? Well, thanks so much. You've been a great consolation. Thank you for the "pep talk", as they say. My wife's a bitch, but it turns out it's all my fault. Great, that's just marvellous. How kind of you to figure it all out for me.'

'How has she sinned against you?'

Nikolai gave a forced laugh.

'Oh, mere trifles. Nothing much. She's a whore, but other than that she's a wonderful woman.'

'Do you mean that she is unfaithful to you?'

'Yes, that is what I mean.'

The priest fell silent for a moment. 'This is a very serious accusation. Are you absolutely sure that it is true? How did you first learn of this?'

The priest looked at him, waiting for an answer. His steady gaze unsettled Nikolai. Suddenly he no longer felt certain of his words.

'I know for sure. People have told me. Yes, I'm certain.' He tried to sound firm.

'Who told you?'

'This man, Bertrand.'

'Who is this Bertrand?'

'My friend.' Nikolai found himself unable to meet the priest's eyes, and this weakness enraged him. 'What difference does it make? It's not as if you know him.'

'What if he's lying? Will you not entertain that possibility? Or perhaps he is simply mistaken.'

'No, no...' Nikolai shook his head, eyes lowered. 'He isn't lying. Unfortunately, he's right. He's always right about everything.'

'Does your wife come to church?'

'I've no idea.'

'When did you last come to church?'

'Not for a long time. I can't remember.' Nikolai forced himself to look the priest in the eyes. 'But what's the point? What is the church actually for?' He and Bertrand had been talking about exactly this a few days earlier, he remembered. 'You ask me when I last came to church as though church attendance is the most important thing in my life. What's a church? Just a house. A building. Like thousands of other buildings. Brick buildings, cement buildings. At best it's a cultural monument, conserved by the government. Mere convention. It has no more to do with God than does a public toilet.'

The priest chuckled. 'Are these your own convictions? Or did someone teach you to think this way?'

Nikolai shrugged. 'Do I need someone to teach me? I'm a big boy, I can think for myself.'

'There's a folk saying, you know. If the Church is not your mother, God cannot be your father.'

'Nonsense. Although... perhaps... I don't want to argue.'

'What I don't understand is why, given your views, you came to this place.'

Nikolai shrugged again.

'I thought someone might help me.'

'But for that, you need to have faith.'

Nikolai gave the priest a long, searching look. 'How did you know she is called Vera?'[1]

'Hmm? Who?'

'My wife.'

The priest chuckled for a second time.

'Just a coincidence. You misunderstood, I meant you must have faith, as in, believe... I wasn't talking about your wife.'

'Oh, I see...'

Nikolai felt awkward; he had no idea what else he could say to the priest.

'Do you really, genuinely want me to try and help you?'

Nikolai shrugged his shoulders, and nodded.

'Bring your wife to me then, and I will talk with her.'

'But what about me, what should I do?' Nikolai didn't try to hide his disappointment. Without knowing it, he had really been hoping for some concrete help, to be shown a way out – but that hadn't happened. He stopped listening to the priest.

'Love and don't lose faith. Care for your wife as Christ cared for the Church – that is the teaching of St. John Chrysostom. Though you might have to surrender your very soul for her sake,

1 As well as being a name, Vera is the Russian word for faith.

to endure many losses and much suffering, you must not turn away. For no sacrifice of yours could come close to the sacrifice that Christ made for the Church... Can you hear me?'

Nikolai nodded, without looking at the priest. His eyes were again on the group of old black-clad women by the doors.

'Let us remember the words of Christ, when they brought the woman before him to be stoned. It was the law then to take a woman accused of adultery, tie her to a post and throw stones until she died. Anyone could cast a stone. And Christ said to them, "He that is without sin among you, let him first cast a stone at her."'

'Yeah, yeah, we know all about it...' The conversation had turned oppressive, and now Nikolai wanted to get away as fast as possible. 'Understood. Noted. Stones and so on... I'm infinitely grateful to you, but I really must get going. I don't have much time left. I'm in a hurry.'

'Come back tomorrow then. Come with your wife.'

'Yes, of course, thank you. We'll definitely both come.' Nikolai almost held out his hand, but thought better of it. No doubt priests didn't do handshakes. They didn't do anything normal and human, he thought bitterly as he made for the exit, his eyes fixed straight ahead.

'We'll bring all our neighbours too!' he shouted back from the doorstep. 'And our friends and relatives! And the whole brass bloody band!'

'Idiot,' he said loudly as soon as he was outside. 'What the bloody hell was that?!'

At the outer gate he turned, without stopping, and spat in the direction of the church.

HOPE

Bertrand laughed like a drain when Nikolai confessed he'd been to church. At first he hadn't believed him, sniggering that Nikolai was pulling his leg, mocking him. Then Bertrand careened around the room, propping himself up on the walls, the wardrobe, as he grew weak with laughter. He threw back his head and brayed, his mouth wide open, hysterical.

'All right, that's enough,' Nikolai told him but Bertrand just laughed even louder.

'Don't talk!' He waved his hands in the air to make it quite clear that a mere word from Nikolai would send him into fresh paroxysms.

Nikolai tried again. 'I don't see what you find so funny about it. So what? I went to church, I talked to a priest...'

At this Bertrand laughed so much he had to crouch low to the floor. Nikolai decided to stay silent.

Finally Bertrand calmed down. He wiped the tears off his face with his hand and sat down opposite Nikolai, looking at him with an expression of cheerful mockery.

'Yep,' he said. 'I wouldn't like to be you. You've got your knickers in a right twist. But I must say, I didn't expect you to be quite such an idiot. I won't deny you're having a hard time, but...'

He raised a finger.

'Do you remember the line, "A man – how glorious, how proud that sounds!"? Now, I know it's a worn-out and clichéd phrase, but still, one mustn't forget it! The man who said it was no fool. You've let yourself go, you've got no control of yourself. Frankly you're turning into a big wet girl. That's right, I said it. What were you thinking? That they were going to pat you on the head, feel sorry for you? Shed some tears, perhaps? Light a candle for you and show you the way?'

Bertrand shook his head at Nikolai.

'It's all just words. You're a man. You were born strong. You were born with power. You've got to use that power, you've got to rule! That's what life means if you're a man. Religion is there to console the losers and the cowards, the cripples and the deformed. Maybe it sounds harsh to put it like that, but it's the simple truth. Who goes to church? People who can't count on themselves, who don't trust their own intelligence and abilities. People who are afraid of life, who get lost in it like stupid lab mice in a maze. You're not like them! Do you understand? You are a person of worth – a man, a king – and all these doubts, tortuous thoughts, sufferings, they're nothing to do with you! Your goal is to exercise your power, to dominate. Those who prevent you or oppose you must be crushed, brought to heel. Of course, if you can't manage that, then...'

'Try to understand...'

Bertrand took both Nikolai's hands in his.

'You know what I'm about to say. It sounds banal, but it has to be said all the same: life is a very cruel game, and there's no room for weak players.'

Nikolai lifted his head to look the man in the eye.

'You think I'm a fool. You think I don't know how you see me? Well, I'm not a fool.' Nikolai shook his head. 'No. I'm no fool. And yet everything is so complicated and painful...'

'Who told you things would be simple?'

'I'm not saying things have to be simple... But I don't have the strength. I just can't, I'm not coping. How can I dominate other people when I can barely look after myself?'

'Now this is no good at all. You started so well, but that last bit is no good at all. Sure, life is difficult – haven't I already said that? – but you have to fight. You can't just give up. Pity is the lowliest of emotions. A strong and healthy person should never feel pity – it's unnatural, a perversion of all normal, healthy laws of life – but self-pity is a thousand times more disgusting! How can you be so pathetic?'

'I don't know,' Nikolai whispered. 'I don't know anything anymore.'

'Well, you ought to know! Who else could possibly know? You are alone in this life, alone against the world. It's a never-ending battle in a never-ending war and no one is going to help you, no one is going to catch you if you trip and fall. On the contrary, everyone will be delighted to see you go down, believe me. Who are people drawn to? Winners, of course! When you're strong and lucky, one victory after another – that's when you have acclaim, your friendship is sought after, you're valued, you're loved. Only then! People gravitate towards strength. They forgive the strong for using their teeth to show dominance and superiority. But they never forgive weakness.'

Nikolai nodded. 'Yes, you're right.'

'Of course I am! But look – I am your friend. Maybe the only person in your life who wants to help you. Who can help you. Why? Just because I can tell you're not like everybody else. I know you better than you know yourself.'

'Fine. You're right. But all this is just...' Nikolai struggled to find the right word. 'It's just theory. There's theory and then there's practice. How do you apply it to life? Everything you're saying makes sense, but...'

'But what?'

'But Vera, for example! I love her. I can't live without her, but I can't live with her either, not like this. Why does she lie to me? Why is she tormenting me like this, mocking me? How can I find a way out? Does a way out even exist?'

Bertrand placed a calming hand on his shoulder.

'Easy now, no need to get upset. And you mustn't shout, it's bad for your vocal chords. Nothing has ever been solved by shouting. You want to find a way out? You want to know if there's a way out?'

'Yes.'

Bertrand gave a gentle, almost patronising smile.

'Of course there's a way out.'

'So what is it?'

'It's very simple. Right now you're weak and open. That's a boxing term, you know, for being unguarded. You leave yourself open, and naturally what follows is a punch. You've ceded ground. Not just that, but you've ceded ground to a woman, who in fact is much weaker than you. But you can't save yourself on your own. You need help. You need a strong arm to lean on, someone to point the way and lead you out. *Trust me and let me help you.*'

Bertrand was very still, his lips barely moving as he spoke in a virtual whisper. His low voice cast a soothing spell over Nikolai, giving him strength and hope.

'We're going to think of this as a chess match: we will lose pieces deliberately in order to win the game. You must get a hold of yourself, learn to be cool, impassive. Most importantly, you have to learn to be observant. To watch and wait. Your time will come. Don't neglect the smallest detail. Her every move and step, her every word – no matter how trivial it might seem – might turn out to be full of significance. In the end your time will come, no doubt about it, and you will pay her back in full.'

After a silence, Bertrand added: 'Then you will learn what it is to be a winner. Don't trust anyone or anything, especially not her. Every word out of her mouth is a lie or a trick or a cover-up. Remember this: right now you've got one friend and ally. Only one. And I am that friend. Believe me.'

Nikolai nodded. He was exhausted. He was barely able to keep his eyes open; his head was so heavy, so heavy. He didn't have the strength to sit in the armchair and face Bertrand, but he hated to show his weakness. Yet it became harder and harder to fight against it. From above he heard Bertrand's voice.

'Are you tired?'

Nikolai forced himself to open his eyes. It was dark and he couldn't see Bertrand.

'You want to sleep?'

Nikolai nodded weakly: 'Yes.'

SPRING

Spring had begun and Vera fell ill. While sweeping the paths in the public park, she had been caught in a downpour. At first she ran a high fever. For days the grey column of mercury seldom dropped below thirty-nine, rising even higher towards forty each evening. Then over a single day it plummeted to below thirty-six and Vera felt even worse than before. Her mother came often, bringing food, different kinds of medicine each time. Nikolai continued to spend his entire pension on vodka. There wasn't enough for anything else.

He had given up opening the curtains in his room. Sometimes Vera got up, against doctor's orders, and stood at the window, leaning heavily on the sill (waiting for someone, Nikolai suspected), or went to the kitchen to quietly cook something, though she herself ate little. They barely spoke. Nikolai had still not forgiven her for what she had put him through at the theatre. Sometimes when she slept Nikolai came out of his room and sat on the sofa beside her, drinking in the sight of her. She was so pale these days, much more than usual, and her face looked almost unreal, glowing faintly in the gloom. Her breathing was all but inaudible – like she wasn't breathing at all. She was even more beautiful now and loving her was even more agonising.

***

Even now, when Vera was confined to the apartment, weak and seriously ill, Nikolai could see that she still had the means to betray him. True, her old friends no longer visited, but what about Bertrand, whom she let kiss her hands when Nikolai was out of the room? And her mother, the old bitch, had every opportunity of slipping Vera notes from her lovers.

So one day, while his wife was busy in the kitchen, Nikolai made a spyhole in his bedroom door with a screwdriver. It was an inspired idea. Now he would be able to watch her secretly all the time, while she thought she was unobserved. Nikolai spent the evening in high spirits, joking around with Bertrand. He even convinced him to down a big shot of vodka, then laughed at Bertrand's reaction as he comically spluttered and screwed up his face.

'What's with that name of yours, actually? It's just so dumb.'

'It's the name my old man gave me. Something wrong with that?'

'No, nothing... Who was he, your old man?'

'Ah, now,' Bertrand threw his head back and laughed. 'Why do you say "was"? He still *is*, there's no *was*!'

'Who *is* he, then?'

'He is a personage of great importance.'

'What does he do?'

'Why do you ask?'

'Just curious.'

'Well, it's a military secret.'

'Does he have power?'

'He has a lot of power. What is it you need?'

'What do I need? Nothing... well, some money would obviously be nice. It's Vera's birthday soon, as you know. I'd like to buy her a nice present. A new pair of shoes, for example. You've seen the state of her old ones.'

'Quite. I'm amazed they don't simply disintegrate as she walks.'

'Exactly!' Nikolai laughed. 'She comes in one day – it's raining so hard she's soaking wet – and she runs straight into the bathroom. I can hear her crying in there, but she's refusing to open the door. She does that a lot, locks herself in the bathroom so I don't see her crying. She can be strange like that. Anyway, she finally opens the door sobbing, poor thing, and shows me her shoe – it's filthy and sodden and the sole is missing. She accidentally stepped into a mud puddle – we've got roadworks all around just now – and left the bottom of her shoe in the mud. She had to come home barefoot.'

'So you, like the gallant knight that you are, went out into the rain...'

'No, no, she went and found it herself. It took ages. I was watching from the window. Passers-by stopped to look at her and some of them laughed at the sight of a woman rooting around in the mud. She took the shoes to the cobbler's but they didn't want to accept them. Nothing left to glue, they told her, buy a new pair. I felt so sorry for her. She had to wear her slippers to go there – she hasn't got anything else except winter boots. But in the end she got them to do it, and they fixed up the shoes for her. They were ready the next day.'

'Very touching. But how on earth does she put up with you? Another woman would have run off with a wealthy man a long time ago. Especially such a beauty.'

Nikolai sighed, poured out the vodka, drank. He agreed. He wanted to howl with despair, frustration, hopelessness.

Bertrand suddenly leapt up and sprang towards the door. How could he know about the spyhole? Nikolai pushed him aside to see for himself. Vera was getting up slowly, supporting herself against the sofa. She put on her dressing gown, slipped her feet into her slippers, and walked away.

THE VISIT

Even though Vera was already feeling much better, it was Nikolai who went to answer the door. He always went himself now – he needed to know for sure who was coming into their house. On the way he glanced at the hallway clock: around two o'clock. He opened the door and at once recognised their visitor. It was the director whose photo he had seen hanging in the theatre next to his wife's. Nikolai even remembered the director's surname. The man greeted him. Nikolai made no reply and let him through, staring gloomily at the floor and slamming the door behind him. The director was saying something but Nikolai waved him away and walked past him to his bedroom. There, he immediately bent to the spyhole in the door.

'Good afternoon,' he heard the man say to Vera in a sonorous and confident theatre voice.

His wife smiled as she raised herself to a sitting position and nodded in reply. It occurred to Nikolai that the blanket could slide down any moment and reveal her breasts (obviously that was exactly what Vera wanted, to show the man her breasts) but instead Vera lay back down and pulled the covers up to her chin.

'Are you unwell?'

Nikolai's wife nodded and smiled again: a cold, flu, complications... Vera spoke very softly and Nikolai now regretted pulling his door firmly shut. He could hardly make out his wife's weak voice.

'I see... I see. And are you taking something?'

'The doctor... herbs... prescriptions... my mother...' Something else Nikolai couldn't make out.

'Perhaps I can help in some way? I have a doctor friend. He's an old man now. He studied in France, his parents were of that first wave of émigrés. He can diagnose over the phone things that others can't figure out with an x-ray right in front of their face. He's a genius, a bona fide genius – and kind too. I'm not exaggerating. He brings patients back from the brink of death. I could call him right now if you like?'

Nikolai strained to decode the hidden meaning of all these words.

'Thank you, I'm most grateful, but my mother... all I need... the doctor... her neighbour...'

Mother, doctor, neighbour... What did it mean?

'How is your temperature?'

'It was very high at first, never dropped under 39... for some time... but now it's gone right down...'

'But that's no good at all. That's worse. I mean, not always of course, but in cases like this. If you're running a high fever it means your body is putting up a fight... But I'm no expert when it comes to medical matters. How do you feel overall?'

'Much better, thank you.'

His wife's voice had grown stronger now, and Nikolai could hear everything from behind the door.

'Well then, thank goodness for that, thank goodness. Everyone sends regards, their warmest wishes.'

Bertrand elbowed him sharply in the side: 'Pay attention now.'

He handed Nikolai a cigarette and clicked his gold lighter. But Nikolai knew without being told that something was about to happen, that now was the time to be especially vigilant and pay attention, not to miss a single word, when each one might conceal some hint, some secret meaning.

'Thank you. Please tell them that I...'

His wife fell silent for a moment, then said: 'Please tell them I'm very touched by their concern.'

'Ira has had her baby.'

'Aha!' Nikolai gave Bertrand a pointed look.

'What did she have?'

'A son.'

'How wonderful. A son...'

Nikolai's chest constricted painfully. His wife lay back and looked up at the ceiling. Were her eyes really red and moist or was he just imagining it?

'Do pass on my congratulations,' Vera said after a long pause. 'Be sure to tell her.'

'Of course I will. And in the summer, we'll all go touring to Moscow.'

His wife was silent.

'And after that, possibly even abroad, though that's still not confirmed. You know the Shakespeare festival? Yes, that very one! We received their official invitation. And the fact is, it's mostly thanks to you, your performance. Remember that video of your performance we sent them? So now, everything depends on...' – the director pointed at the ceiling – 'whatever they decide upstairs. But we're all keeping our fingers crossed.'

'I'll keep my fingers crossed too.'

'Wonderful.'

Nikolai didn't see the director striding about the room so much as hear him. Through the hole only the sofa and his wife were visible. The man could well be signalling to her from the far side of the room, out of sight. Nikolai's legs were falling asleep. He hopped noiselessly back from the door and returned with a chair. Much more comfortable.

'Tell me,' his wife said almost inaudibly, 'how is Petya?'

He's all right,' the director answered, also lowering his voice. 'He's back to work already.'

Nikolai was taking long, furious drags of his cigarette. It trembled between his fingers.

'Send him my regards too,' said Vera, all but in a whisper.

'Of course... You know, he doesn't hold it against you. If that's the right phrase. He was in a terrible state, hideous.' The director was almost whispering. 'At first everyone thought he'd be crippled for life. That he might never walk again. He was very brave through it all, not everyone could recover from something like that. Multiple bone fractures. Crushed jaw. Shattered vertebrae. His front teeth knocked out altogether... Well, what can you say.'

'Yes,' said his wife. 'Let's not talk about it anymore.'

They were silent. Nikolai flicked the ash straight onto the floor.

'I think about you all a lot... Who is playing Liza now?'

The director told her some name that was meaningless to Nikolai. He heard how the man sat down in the armchair.

'May I smoke?'

'Of course, go ahead...'

'It won't bother you? In your condition?'

Nikolai got up, poured himself a drink, bolted it and sat down again.

'You must know why I've come to see you.'

His wife didn't say a word. She only turned away, lay down again and fixed her gaze on the ceiling.

'I would like to know how final your decision truly is. Tell me honestly, could you really give up acting for good? You have a gift! I just can't believe you'd give it all up. It makes no sense at all!'

'My decision is final,' Vera said, after some time.

'Listen to me!' The director sprang up from his seat and began to pace the room. 'Can you really have no idea what you mean to the company? Our entire repertoire has gone to the dogs without you. Everything was riding on you! Believe it or not, I never understood that before. It was all going so well, so smoothly. Everyone in the troupe liked you, the public adored you. You see, you're not just another actress, you've somehow become the main event, the talk of our town. I know it's hard for you to see it. Do you remember Pushkin's lines about the fleeting apparition, the genius of pure beauty? That's you! In our small, provincial, mediocre grey town, *you* have become that "genius of pure beauty"! People weren't just coming to the theatre, they were coming to see *you*, to enjoy – no, that's not the right word... to be touched by your great gift, your marvellous beauty, your pureness, and everything that defines you and that I can't find the words for, not being Pushkin after all. And now you've quit the theatre. Without a word of warning, I might add. I can't sleep at night, thinking how to fix this. Of course we've got others to take your roles, but Lord knows, even they can tell, poor creatures, that they can't pull it off, that they don't even come close to you. They're not even pale copies of you, they're more like – this is between us, I'd get eaten alive if anyone heard me say it – they're like caricatures of you... A genius like yours, can't you see, is impossible to replace. Your quitting the company is more than just a huge loss for us, it's a death sentence! I know that sounds dramatic, but I mean it. You are so young, barely in your twenties, and you're just setting out, and you've got a future ahead of you that fills me with delight for you, and anxiety, and I'll admit it, envy, too. Look, if everything works out, this summer we could be performing at the Shakespeare festival, where impresarios and critics and producers and theatre people from all around the world come to find new talent. They can't fail to notice you. You needn't give a shit about the troupe, but think about yourself at least. It's all yours for the taking. The sky's the limit! How can you be so foolish and throw it all away?'

'It isn't foolish at all,' Vera said firmly, but Nikolai could tell she could barely hold back the tears.

'But why, goddamn it, why do you have to quit entirely? Can you explain that to me at least?'

'I can...' Vera began, but the man cut her off.

'All right, I know very well why, but listen...' He went up to the sofa and continued in a softer voice. Nikolai could only see his legs. 'You are doing this because of your husband, so much is clear. There are no other reasons. Am I right?'

Vera said nothing.

'Let's be honest with one another. We are not children. You are afraid of him. Am I right? If you let me, I will go in to him right now and talk to him man-to-man, make him see sense. You are destroying your own life. I can't stand by and watch it happen.'

'No, don't even think of doing that.'

'God in heaven, I don't understand you at all. What is this, serfdom? The Middle Ages? It would be funny if it wasn't so awful! So your husband is an imbecile, or a dangerous madman, but why should everyone around him have to suffer?'

Nikolai saw his wife raise herself on her elbows and sit up. Her eyes were wide and dark with indignation.

'Not another word! You should be ashamed. You have no idea what you're talking about. You don't know him. It's the only reason I can forgive you for what you've just said about him. You have no idea what he's suffered, not the smallest idea! You can't understand why I quit? You think I'm afraid, or bound to him like a serf? On your own conscience be all the things you've just said. I know... I know you're trying to help me, but... all these words... there is nothing in the world, nothing – how can I explain? – these things – career, public opinion, art, people, ideals – none of them are worth an iota of what he means to me, they couldn't replace even the smallest part of him. You can call it what you want, and think of me what you like...'

She burst into tears, hiding her face in her hands.

There could no longer be any doubt. Vera had sat up on the bed so that the covers could – as though by accident, as though she were overcome by sincere emotion and didn't notice – fall away to reveal her neck and bosom. Nikolai waited, strained to the limit, ready to burst into the room and catch her at it. It was imperative to wait for the right moment, when it would be too late for them to make excuses. But for some reason Vera lay down again and pulled up the covers, gazing once more at the ceiling. The director still stood beside the sofa.

'But how can you excuse his behaviour that awful night?'

'He thought I was naked,' Nikolai heard her say. 'Naked on the stage.'

***

Again the black sphere stood before his eyes, just as it had at the theatre. Nikolai jumped up and staggered blindly around the room. He bumped into the table by the window, took a few deep breaths, then came to himself and returned to his chair.

He was no longer listening to the voices behind the door, and anyway they now sounded calm and placid, talking about the weather, or health matters, or the apartment. But he knew they would never be able to trick him again. He had only to watch and wait.

***

So it began.

They grew quiet, then started talking again. But he could see, he could clearly see through the spyhole how the covers were lifted up and a hand began to caress her leg, wandering higher and higher with every stroke. Nikolai could barely hold himself in check. He urged himself to wait a little more, just a second more! – and then, then the covers were dispensed with, and there lay Vera, naked, her eyes closed, her head thrown backwards, her pale, long, slender body blending with the white sheets.

At that very moment Nikolai flung open the door and, carrying a chair by the legs, came into the room.

They say they searched for Bertrand for a long time in the tunnel, since there was no way out of it at all, there was no possible escape, no exit – it was a blind tunnel he had walked into, where his heavy tread echoed loudly in the darkness.

They say that the man in charge of his execution was later found dead in his own home, lying with his veins slashed in a bath with no water. His face looked gruesome, blue-tinged with bulging eyes and a gaping mouth that seemed to the people who had gathered around him to want to say something, as though any moment now the lips would move and everyone would hear his words. It was horrible to stand next to the bath filled with clotted blood and to look upon this body, all but unrecognisable as a person who had so recently been their commander.

It was strange, but the people who had been in the underground tunnel that day perished one after another, and before long, within only a few scant months, not one was left alive. Not one remained of those who had walked Bertrand down the stairs into the dark cellar – of those who had shut the heavy metal door behind him, of those who had stood afterwards, listening to that heavy, confident, measured tread which echoed loudly in the darkness.

HOSPITAL

Due to a shortage of beds, alcoholics – among whom Nikolai was counted – were placed in ward 21, where the genuine madmen lay. There were only a few of these madmen, all quiet people, and to Nikolai's surprise there seemed no way to tell them apart from normal, sane people. Except for the unbelievably thin man, tall as a basketball player, who wandered around with his head firmly pressed to his right shoulder, springing on his toes with each step and endlessly droning a strange tune in his deep, unpleasant bass: 'ya-ya-doo, ya-ya-doo, ya-ya-doo' – always with the emphasis on the last 'doo'. This man did have the scary face of an idiot.

Three times a day, in the morning, at noon and in the evening, they sedately took their meals, served on tin crockery in the small communal cafeteria. Their treatments and rare visits by indifferent doctors they received with equal composure. At the scheduled time they went out for a walk, and every day except Sunday they made a visit to the single-story wooden workshops outside for what was termed 'work therapy', which the alcoholics never did.

The alcoholics were supposed to sleep on mattresses laid out on the floor in the dormitory's gangways, but every night at lights out, when only two orderlies were supervising the ward, they would turf the lunatics out of their metal cots (whose legs were screwed into the floor) and sleep there themselves until morning. The orderlies disliked the madmen, despising them from the bottom of their soul, so they turned a blind eye.

His wife was not allowed to visit him in the hospital, and as he lay on his mattress or paced the corridors window to window, Nikolai thought endlessly of her. He could see now that he had acted like a mere boy that day, foolishly and impulsively, and as a result he was now locked up in this hospital no different than a prison while Vera could receive whomsoever she pleased at home with the minimum of fuss. She would hardly care what the neighbours thought. She had probably gone back to the theatre by now, stripping naked every night before hundreds of eyes. That balding old connoisseur of nudity, he was sure to be gawping at her breasts again through his opera glasses. Nikolai could still hear his drooling whisper, the moronic way he kept saying 'bosoms'.

***

Two months ago the alcoholics had come up with a diverting gag, which they repeated every three or four days. There was an old man on the ward, small and bow-legged, who resembled a boy with rickets. A veteran of the ward, he had been there for years: he had strangled his own daughter after finding a roll-up cigarette in her pocket. Alone among the patients, he talked a great deal and quite sensibly. He was quick to laugh, always holding on to his belly while he did so, as though something was about to fall out. And he was exceedingly neat and tidy, even washing the alcoholics' undergarments on his own initiative.

The gag consisted of the old man springing out of the ward into the corridor just as a female orderly passed by. He then grabbed her backside and pressed himself against it, roaring with laughter and shouting, 'The worm wants into his worm-hole!' This caused great hilarity among the assembled company.

Each and every time this happened, the old woman would turn around and give him a sharp punch in the stomach with her bony fist, then knee him in the balls, whereupon the old man fell over, clutching at the wall and choking as he writhed on the floor with his toothless mouth wide open. Nor was this by any means the end of the thrilling spectacle. The orderly would call her colleagues, who chased down the old man (if by that time he happened to have recovered and was running away in the vain hope of escaping his pursuers). Otherwise they would simply lift him off the floor and throw him onto his cot, where he pumped his arms and legs, reminding Nikolai of a beetle accidentally turned onto its back. Then they would flip him onto his stomach and jab four extremely painful 'orderly shots' (as they were called in hospital jargon) through his clothes – two in the arse and two beneath the shoulder blades. The old fool would spend a couple of hours screaming without cease. He couldn't get out of bed on his own. At night he had to be carried into the toilets, otherwise his moans and groans kept everyone awake. Then the next day they would heave him out of bed, hoisting him upright onto the floor and shoving him in the back to force him to take a step, as a result of which the pain, having subsided a little during the night, would return with fresh force. For two or three days the old man couldn't bend at all, but moved around with his body held completely straight as though it had been lashed to an invisible board by an invisible rope. The alcoholics joked that he looked like a soldier on those days, with that incredibly upright bearing. And that's what they called him, by the way – the soldier. Eventually the pain would fade and all would be forgotten. And so the marvellous joke was repeated again, and amused the men just as much as the first time.

LEONID

One day when they were led out into the stone-walled inner courtyard for their walk, Nikolai spotted a newbie. Strangely, the man was wearing his own clothes – jeans and a t-shirt – instead of hospital clothing, nor had they cut his hair, as they did here with everyone. Keeping apart from the others, he moved slowly about the yard, intently scrutinising the men's faces. When he saw Nikolai in the corner, leaning back against a tree, the man stopped in his tracks and walked over with a smile.

'Hello there,' he said. Nikolai liked him straight-away. There was a charm to his kind, cultured face and his pleasant, engaging way of talking.

'Hello.'

'What a beautiful sky we have today.'

Nikolai looked up.

'It's ok.'

The man fell silent for a time then suddenly asked: 'Tell me, are you sick? I mean, mad?'

Nikolai shook his head no.

The man let out a sigh of relief, then chuckled apologetically.

'Forgive the dumb question. Frankly it's a bit scary to be in a place like this for the first time. You don't know who is safe to talk to, or how you should talk, or whether there's any use in talking at all! All kinds end up here, you know? One of them might just hurl himself at you and bite. I'm joking, of course,' he laughed, and gave a shake of the head to flick the hair from his brow. 'But you know what I mean, right?'

Nikolai nodded. 'Of course.'

'Oh, that's great. I honestly didn't think I'd find a person in here that I could just talk to. Again, forgive me, but I have to tell you that I liked you straight-away. As soon as I saw you, it was like something prodded me, telling me here's someone you can approach, here's a good person.' He looked happily into Nikolai's face as he spoke.

'Thank you.'

'And you know, we should probably stick together. You never know what might happen, I feel like a round peg in a square hole here, so to speak. But with you I'll feel better. Have you been here long?'

'Not really.'

'It must be very tedious?'

'It's not exactly a riot.'

'Oh...' The man seemed upset. 'No matter, no matter... I know a lot of jokes, I'll entertain you. And just between ourselves, I...' – he looked around and whispered in Nikolai's ear – 'I've brought a pack of cards from home. They won't confiscate them, will they?'

Nikolai shrugged. What did it matter?

'So we'll have enough to keep ourselves amused. My name is Leonid, by the way.' He extended his hand and Nikolai shook it.

'Nikolai.'

***

They were called in to lunch. On their way up to the first-floor ward, Nikolai had a strange urge to tell everything to this man who laughed so cheerfully and listened with such attention. He would surely understand, and maybe he would pity him...

No, that didn't matter. It wasn't pity Nikolai wanted, but someone to unburden himself onto. Aside from Bertrand he had never told a soul about what was happening between him and Vera, and it was such a long time since he had seen Bertrand.

After they had finished lunch and washed their hands, greasy from touching the dishes, they settled on his mattress and Nikolai started talking.

The sick joke of it – that was how he began his story – was that he loved her. He was genuinely, hopelessly in love with his wife. If not for that, Nikolai would have divorced her long ago. He would never live with a woman who deceived him at every turn, who cheated on him, who took her clothes off in the theatre for all to see, who constantly lied to him, and who, even in their very home, with him just on the other side of the wall, shamelessly entertained her lover. 'You tell me, tell me, how is it even possible?!' Nikolai clutched his head. He was talking loudly, not thinking about the fact that others could hear him. It would have been easier to kill himself, yes, hanging himself would have been a thousand times more pleasant, a joy and a delight compared to what he had endured with the endless strange phone calls, the insinuations of house guests, and her, naked at the theatre, day after day! He had to watch it happen under his nose and bear it all. But not because he was a coward. He just needed to know for sure that his suspicions were not baseless, before he took measures. In the end she had even entertained her lover while he was there. In their apartment.

Nikolai sprang up from the mattress, then dropped back again. He had not yet had the chance to tell anyone what had happened on that day he'd caught them at it, his wife and the director. How sorry he was that he'd only managed to hit the man a few times before Vera screamed and threw herself at him, hanging on Nikolai's neck in an attempt to protect her lover. That was what really had set Nikolai off – that she had thrown herself on him to try to shield her lover. His first blow knocked her down. She screamed as he struck her cheeks again and again; beside himself, he began to kick her, which he had never allowed himself to do before. Why now? Because of how brazenly, how blatantly she had betrayed him in defending her lover. The lover, taking advantage of the fact that Nikolai had forgotten about him, fled without Nikolai even registering his disappearance.

The entire aftermath was muddled and vague, eluding his memory. Everything went black, then his wife suddenly vanished too, and Nikolai was hacking at the sofa with an axe. The wire mattress coils, denuded of their coverings, seemed alive; they twitched and wriggled like worms, latching onto his hands and shirtsleeves, twitching, wriggling... It was disgusting, his body twisted with revulsion, and as he ran from the apartment, afraid he would fall into the midst of all that writhing living blackness, he was suddenly thrown to the ground, beaten, tied up...

He could no longer speak. He squeezed his eyes shut and covered his face with his hands, leaning back against a cot on which a man in blue hospital pyjamas lay still as a corpse.

Nikolai opened his eyes to find Leonid looking at him brightly.

'Do you want me to lift you? Do you want me to lift you up to the ceiling?' He prodded Nikolai to his feet.

'Just stand still, stand right there,' Leonid went on, 'and focus.'

Leonid took a few steps back, pushing his long black hair from his forehead, took a deep breath, and put his hands out slowly, fingers splayed. His face strained and went red. Breathing heavily, he stared without blinking, his lips tightly pressed.

'Can you feel yourself lifting from the floor? Can you? Don't be alarmed, I'll stop you before you hit the ceiling.'

Not quite recovered from telling his story, Nikolai suddenly realised that he had seen this man somewhere before. He strained to remember where and when.

At last Leonid relaxed his stance and let his hands drop, breathing normally again. He clenched and unclenched his fingers, strong and attractive like those of a pianist, and walked up to Nikolai with a smile.

'Well? How did it feel? I'm not quite myself today as you can see, I only managed a couple of centimetres. But it's not a bad beginning. I started out small, with matchboxes and things like that... I remember how astounded they all were the first time I managed to lift a truck. Can you imagine their astonishment? Picture a perfectly unremarkable man walking along the pavement. That would be me. And a truck rolling down the road beside him. This great lumbering vehicle. The man suddenly stops, focuses his mind, eyes half-closed just so – and the truck floats into the air! What a lot of noise they made, so much cheering, especially the children... Yes, sir. Anyway, if you'd like, I can lift you again – though I have to admit it will be more difficult to do it a second time.'

He stuck out his right thumb, squeezing the other fingers into a fist, and waggled it at Nikolai. 'It gets in the way, otherwise I could lift you in one fell swoop to the ceiling. I have it from Openka, you see, and Openka's thumbs are always a bit weak.'

As he looked at the man – his slender frame, his long black hair that curled a little at the ends – and especially as he listened to his curiously genial, spell-binding voice, Nikolai remembered when and where he had seen him before. He remembered everything now. For a moment he felt pure terror.

'Enough. I know who you are now,' Nikolai stuck out his hand and pointed his finger at him. 'I saw you.'

Leonid fell silent at once and looked shiftily around, but there was no one in the ward apart from the pyjama-clad man, who still lay unmoving in his cot.

'All right, but what of it?' Leonid smiled. It seemed a somewhat tired smile, tired and a little rueful. 'I remembered you too. It just took a while.'

'Wait,' said Nikolai. He was trying to make sense of his memories, which were agonisingly vague, viscous... 'But wasn't it...? I always thought that was a dream.'

Still smiling, Leonid looked at him silently.

'It was a dream, right? I saw you in my dream?'

Leonid nodded.

'Yes, it was only a dream.'

'But how did you recognize me?' said Nikolai. 'I was just a boy then... I was only seven or eight years old, nine at the most. Surely I must have changed?'

Leonid nodded again. 'You have. And yet I knew you right away. Something of that little boy is still in there, though it's true you have changed. The same features maybe? And that scar of course...'

THE SCAR

'I didn't have the scar back then,' said Nikolai. 'That happened about five years ago.'

'Is that all? Well, in that case I don't know.'

They were silent for a time.

'It's too bad, I shouldn't have approached you. I ought to have thought about it first. That's just like me, I don't think things through and later I regret it.'

'Wait... wait. Didn't you hang yourself?!'

The terror was on him again. Something was happening to the eyes of the man standing before him. Nikolai saw them change hue – darker and darker they grew, and when Leonid spoke again they were entirely black. To Nikolai it seemed they were not eyes at all, just two round holes, and beyond them something black as night, a totality of blackness.

'Did you see me hang myself?'

'No, but that's what everyone was saying.'

'Was everyone saying that?' Leonid smiled. 'Yes, I suppose everyone was talking about it. It was quite an affair.'

'So did you hang yourself or not?'

'How persistent you are... and tactless, for that matter.'

Leonid sat down on the cot.

'Honestly, what difference does it make? Yes, all right, I hanged myself.'

Nikolai did not hear his answer. He was already thinking of something else.

'Why did you kill her?'

'Now isn't the time to...'

Leonid didn't have a chance to finish. Nikolai leapt on him, grabbed him by the collar and shook him roughly.

'Why did you do it?! Why did you kill her?!' shouted Nikolai. 'I saw the whole thing! I was there, I know it was you!'

Leonid did not resist, and soon Nikolai let go.

'How can you possibly know that, if I don't know anything myself?' Leonid sounded weak and tired and sad.

The man in the cot, without opening his eyes, pronounced loudly and clearly: 'Give it to me! Gimme!'

In unison they turned their heads to him, but the man fell silent as suddenly as he had piped up.

'How can I explain to you? It's all so complicated... I was a perfectly ordinary, normal man. Until I saw *her*. And then everything changed, the world flipped on its axis, and everything was inside out. It sounds clichéd, I know, but that's exactly how it was.

'I had finished school and started college like everyone else, and was a fairly diligent student, actually. I mean, I wasn't especially hard-working *per se*, but I went to nearly all the lectures, did the usual stupid essays, gave talks at seminars... Once I even went to some sort of conference.

'I did have girls, you know. Relationships, crushes... Even love, or what seemed like love... Girls liked me, but that wasn't the point of life for me, you know? Girls, love, none of that was essential. Not that I gave it much thought, what was essential. Life just went on, and I just went on too... until I saw *her*, our mutual acquaintance, and everything shifted. In a single day. It was a kind of madness... it *was* madness. Insanity.

'I was going home from my girlfriend's. I remember it was very hot and I was walking slowly: it was hard to move at all, the air was so sweltering you could hardly breathe. And so I was walking, and then I heard loud voices, then blaring laughter. I turned around and looked up. There were people standing on a balcony, two men, or perhaps three. It was their laughter I'd heard. I caught a glimpse of something falling, but couldn't tell what. There was a boy sitting beside the entrance. That was you.

'And then I saw her coming out of the front door. My first thought was that I had sun-stroke. I felt faint and dizzy with fear – I was that kind of over-sensitive young man. Yes, when I saw she was naked, I decided I must have sun-stroke. You remember, I'm sure. But I quickly realised she was drunk, it was obvious from the unsteady way she walked, barely able to keep to her feet. This was a relief, somehow, because it was an explanation. She almost fell, but just managed to hold on to the wall, and stay on her feet.

'It was all pretty sordid and shameful: a drunken girl, her leering, skanky, drunken pals – I had twigged by then that it was her clothes they'd thrown off the balcony. There was no reason to stay and watch. I should have kept walking. But I suddenly felt I couldn't leave. I don't know how to explain it. I couldn't even bring myself to look away.'

Head hung low, Leonid sat looking at the floor for a long time.

'I couldn't look at anything but her, or think of anything else. I drank in every movement, every line and curve of her body... It's hard to talk about it. Impossible to explain how I felt or describe how I saw her. She drove me mad. I had never seen anything like it.

'I stayed there long after she'd gone back inside. Then I realised that I was ridiculous, that they were watching me and laughing at me – the men on the balcony were still there – and I forced myself to walk away. But from that moment, I couldn't think of anything but her. How bitterly I regretted, afterwards, that I hadn't followed her up to that squalid apartment. I'm sure they would have let me in. Who knows, perhaps my desire would have passed completely, or at least ceased to be such a torment.

'I carried on going to lectures, seeing my friends, talking to my parents; I ate and slept and woke up at the appropriate times. There was no external change. To everyone around me I was probably the same as always. Not one of them could have imagined how false and artificial my life had become. The only genuine, truthful thing in my life was what I felt for her, though I was scared to acknowledge it even to myself, and tried to hide it. I needed her, I had to see her. But I had no idea who she was. I would have sold my soul. I wanted her. She was so beautiful.

'I noticed you right away, following her around the whole time. It was a bloody nuisance, really annoyed me.

'The truth is, I was quite shy back then. I rarely made the first move with a girl; it all seemed to happen on its own, almost in spite of me. And so now I was at a loss. I don't know how I would have managed it if I hadn't met this man... It was only thanks to him. He knew just what to do, he was an expert, you see, and had a cool head. He was wise. He told me how to go about it, and it turned out to be a piece of cake.'

Leonid grinned. 'She was... she was beautiful as a goddess and available as the ultimate whore. She just loved to go with men. And so we met, and got to know each other, and everything came together pretty fast. It turned out she was about to graduate from high school, and lived with her parents who, as luck would have it, had just come home from their holidays. So we couldn't go to hers. We decided we'd go to the park that evening instead. She had no qualms, believe me. She would have been up for doing it in the stairwell.

'I had the sense that you were always knocking about, just out of sight. But that night I didn't give a shit. We went to the park and she led me to some corner where there were no street-lights and it was dark (I'm sure it wasn't her first time there). We sat down. She was laughing all the time. I talked and she laughed, and her laughter drove me wild. She had these big white teeth and they flashed, even in the dark. For some reason I thought they must be very sharp. Big, white and sharp. I kissed her and kissed her, but she only laughed and she let me do anything I wanted. We had hardly known each other a day. The sensation was extraordinary. I stroked her darling little legs, I stroked them and nibbled them... just nipped them here and there, lightly, softly, tenderly, and she loved that, the sensuous little creature...

'At some point I lost my head completely. I can't explain what came over me. It was like a wave carrying me forward. Like a current, you know? I wasn't really doing anything, it was all just happening of its own accord. Probably I was too aroused, it was too much for me. The waiting for that day had been so intense. Something happened to me. I was out of my mind, not myself. It sounds stupid. I was doing strange things, things I'd never even imagined. She suddenly started screaming. That's the last thing I remember.

'And another thing – it was pitch black, but all at once I could see as if it were daylight.

'I only came to my senses once I was back at home. I stood in the bathroom, in front of the mirror, but there – in the glass opposite me – stood a completely different person. You can't imagine how terrifying that is. In that moment I knew I had gone mad. Then the reflection began to change, and my features began to appear in the person facing me. I turned away for a second, I don't know why – probably from sheer fright – and when I looked into the mirror again, everything was fine, I had my own face back. Everything would have been wonderful if it hadn't been for the blood on my hands. I hadn't noticed it before. Blood on my shirt too. I was drenched in it. Not just that, I was barefoot and my feet were also covered in blood.

'Then I started to piece things together, my memory was gradually returning. I wish it hadn't. I couldn't bear remembering. And besides, I was sure now that you had seen everything. I had no choice but to kill myself.'

Leonid fell silent. Nikolai remained silent as well. They didn't look at one another. Finally, Nikolai broke the silence.

'So you came here to tell me all about it.'

Turning to him, Leonid shook his head.

'No. That's not it. Why would I? You know the whole story already. It was just that... Your wife, Vera, she looks so much like that girl. She is so very beautiful...'

'What does my wife have to do with you?' Nikolai suddenly felt rage. 'Nobody's asking you about my wife!'

Leonid did not seem to hear him.

'It's important, what I'm trying to tell you, so try to understand. Vera is her sister – not a blood sister of course... No, I'm not saying it right. She...'

Nikolai jumped towards him, his lips trembling.

'Not one more word! Don't you say another word!'

Leonid grinned.

'Calm down, I don't mean any offence. I'm talking about something else entirely. You want to know whose face I saw in the mirror that night? All I want is to warn you, to help you if it's not too late, so stop interrupting me and try to understand. Now I don't know if this is something I heard, or if I made it up myself, but here goes... Beauty is the visible incarnation of goodness. You, with your own hands, are helping him to destroy beauty, and with it the fragment – however small – of good that she personifies, the love she has brought with her into the world. I can see you have no idea what I'm talking about. How can I make you understand? They are both beautiful. I only called them sisters because of that. One of them is no more. Let us admit that she participated to the best of her feeble abilities in the destruction of her great gift, but yours – yours is different, completely different...'

Nikolai raised his arm to strike. 'Silence! I said not another word about Vera!'

Choking with rage, he couldn't shout anymore. He had only breath enough for a strangled whisper.

***

Suddenly Nikolai heard laughter behind him. He spun around, hand still raised for the blow. There in the doorway stood his blue-clad fellow patients, a crowd of them freshly returned from lunch. One of them was pointing at Nikolai and, through his laughter, tried to shout down the rest.

'He's gone batshit crazy! That's the medical term – batshit! Look, our man's shitting bats! He's chatting away to himself! Nurse, we need urgent therapy, pronto! He's gone totally batshit!'

Nikolai looked back to where Leonid had stood, but no one was there. There was no one before him in the narrow walk space between the two cots. Nikolai shut his eyes tight then opened them again: there was only the grey-painted wall, and the cots on either side. Strapped to the frame of one cot lay a man in blue hospital pyjamas. Nikolai crouched down and looked at his face; the man's eyes had rolled back in his head and he was breathing noisily and heavily. His bitten tongue lolled to one side along a long unshaven cheek... The merriment behind Nikolai's back continued unabated. Nikolai sprang to his feet, turned around and walked towards the men in the doorway. Taking a short swing, he struck the one who had called him batshit.

The blow hit his throat, and at that very moment everyone fell silent. In the silence one could hear the terrible wheeze of the choking man. He lost consciousness almost immediately, but continued to stand in front of Nikolai, held up by the armpits by those who stood behind him.

'Who's next?' Nikolai asked everyone.

Answer came there none.

THE TALK

'What is it you do exactly? Your profession? If you don't mind saying.'

'I work at the theatre.' The woman had turned to face him. Her eyes were dark and impassioned. 'I'm an actress. I mean, at the moment I work elsewhere – I've quit the theatre – but I trained as an actress.'

He ran an eye over her figure, lingering a moment at the legs, then looked her in the eye again.

'I see, I see. And so you...'

'Yes,' she said firmly. 'I want to take him out of here. To take my husband home. I was told I have the right to do that.'

The woman was finding it hard to read the chief physician, or gauge his reaction to her request. His look was steady and calm and he sat without a word, looking her over unceremoniously. The woman was beginning to feel anxious.

'May I smoke?' she asked while she took a packet of cigarettes from her small black purse.

'Yes, of course. Here you are.' He held out a gold lighter to her where she sat tensely in the corner of a vast antique black sofa, and clicked it. A neat, barely visible column of flame rose above the lighter and licked gently at the cigarette. The woman took a deep drag and leaned back into the sofa. She looked out of the window, where pines formed a solid, dark, green-brown wall. Taking advantage of her wandering attention, the man looked at her bare neck and shoulders, her bright, sensuous lips, her fingers, that trembled slightly each time she brought the cigarette to her lips to inhale deeply.

'So then,' he asked for the umpteenth time 'you'd like to take your husband away from us? Is that...?'

'Yes,' the woman cut in. 'Don't I have every right to do so?'

'We all have every right to do anything we like,' he said, and smiled softly, sweetly. 'Tell me, when did you first notice his... let's call it, his odd behaviour?'

The woman shrugged. Ash fell and shattered silently on her black skirt.

'What do you mean?'

'Angry outbursts, paranoia? Cruelty?'

The woman shrugged again: she didn't know.

'I didn't notice it. Rather, I tried not to notice it. And later I thought it would pass, that it would all turn out all right somehow.'

'Right.'

'I know, I know...' The woman got up from the sofa and, agitated, began to pace the room. 'I know. I understand that I'm to blame for all this. I should have left the theatre at the beginning, when it was just beginning. Everything would have turned out differently...'

'Do sit down,' he said gently.

'Yes, yes – thank you.'

The woman sat down, touched her cigarette to the ashtray.

'I want to take him home. He'll feel better at home. He'll come back to his senses more easily.'

She suddenly began to speak passionately. 'Just give me an answer! Something definite! Can I? Can I take him home or not? Do I have the right? Here, look,' she was fumbling with her handbag. 'He writes letters to me. He's perfectly sane. He's recovered. It's all over, all of *that*.'

Finally she managed to prise open the bag and take out an envelope.

'Look, he writes that he understands what has been happening, that he was ill, that he is very sorry – and he can see clearly that his suspicions were unfounded, that it was his illness that made him think so – his alcoholism, ultimately. Yes, he admits that. He tells me so, and he asks to be forgiven! He understands that he was ill – are you even listening to me? Yes, he was ill, but now he is better, all is well now. He is recovered. He is begging me, like a child!'

The man nodded in agreement and smiled understandingly – a wise, tranquil smile.

'Do you love your husband?'

'What a strange question...' She went quiet for a moment. 'Yes, of course. I love him. Very much.'

He lit up and tossed the gold lighter on his desk, then made a turn about the room, struggling to conceal his own excitement. Standing behind her, he gazed at her neck for a while. For some reason, it was her neck that aroused him most.

'Very much,' he echoed her last words.

'Very much,' she said quietly. But she didn't turn to look at him.

'Forgive me, but I simply don't understand why you're so keen to take him out of our hospital.'

'Because I love him.'

'Love can be blind, you know...'

'Nevertheless.'

'What can I possibly say? You ask too much. I'm afraid I don't want that kind of responsibility. I don't have any reason at all why I should risk my career for your husband.'

He paused, then said pointedly: 'I hope you understand what I mean.'

'But he isn't ill anymore! Why can't you understand? Look, here are the letters, read for yourself...'

He cut the woman off. 'Oh, they all write letters! About how much they've recovered, how wonderful they feel, how they're completely aware of their bad behaviour and how sorry they are for all they've done and all they didn't do. I'll tell you another thing: there isn't one patient here, not one, who really thinks they're sick. I would even call that the principal symptom of their illness. So don't deceive yourself. And forget about deceiving me. Your husband is ill, and it would be rash to discharge him in his condition. It just so happens that in this hospital a certain responsibility rests on my shoulders, and were I to make the decision you so forcefully insist upon, I could be liable for gross misconduct. This is no joke. Why should I break the law? Tell me, what for? Give me a single, sensible reason!'

The woman stared at the floor at her feet, her eyes brimming. The parquet seemed to shift and sway.

'My husband is not ill,' she said, trying to hold back tears. 'He is not ill. Perhaps you're right, perhaps all the others are really ill, but not him. He is only tired. He needs rest, that's all. But he is perishing here, he tells me so in his letters. He can't stay here anymore. He will die here. He's already dying, I can feel it! And so I beg you, take pity on him! Why is it necessary for him to be here, in this frightful hospital?'

'Now you're going to tell me it's like a prison,' he sneered.

'Yes, that's right... That's exactly what I wanted to say. It does look like a prison. Even I feel terrible here, even I feel terrified, walking around these corridors. And these windows that you can't see out of, all of them barred... Why? A person could lose their mind just being here.'

'A sane person could, sure. But everyone in here is not sane. And that's the special nature of this establishment. You talk about losing your mind but – forgive me for being blunt – what mind do our patients have left to lose?'

'I'm not talking about them, I'm only talking about my husband. He is a normal person, completely sound!'

'Really, now?' He smiled, arching his eyebrows to indicate astonishment. 'A completely sound person who beats other persons half to death and takes an axe to his own furniture? I've been a psychiatrist for some time, but I must say that's a new one.'

He went back to his swivelling armchair and flicked his cigarette over the bronze ashtray.

'I beg you. I am a woman, begging you. *I am to blame* for his pain. He loves me. He can't live without me. He is succumbing, I can feel it.' The woman turned to the window, sobbing. 'He is dying and it's my fault. I can't bear it...'

He got up, poured her a glass of water from a carafe and handed it to her.

'Drink this and calm yourself. There's no need to be so upset.'

The woman took a few sips and returned the glass to the table without looking. Wiping her tears, she looked up into his face with a new hope.

'Frankly, what you say isn't without a grain of truth. Your husband has a rather delicate psychological make-up. Indeed, our somewhat, uh, gloomy hospital might do him harm. Possibly, even great harm.'

The woman looked at him in dismay.

'Do you understand me?' he went on.

The woman nodded yes.

'Do you *really* understand me? I feel you don't quite get what I'm saying to you.'

'Do you want money?' With these words the woman blushed and lowered her eyes, then immediately looked up again to the man who sat opposite her, behind the desk, in his white lab coat. 'How much? I'll bring you whatever amount you say.'

He got up, walked to the window, stood at the window sill for a while, then – as if lost in thought about her words, absent-mindedly – went to the door and locked it inaudibly.

'Do you really... *really* want to save your husband?'

'Yes. Yes, I'll do whatever it takes.'

'Whatever it takes?' He repeated her words meaningfully.

'Anything you want,' she said quickly and fervently. 'I'll get together any sum, no matter how much. And I swear, and I swear on what I hold most sacred, that not a living soul will ever know about it. I swear to you.'

So ardent, so tearful and fragile, and so entirely in his power... She was even more attractive, even more beautiful.

'That's good.' He stopped at the sofa, his knees all but touching her legs. 'But I'm not talking about money, my dear, that's the thing.'

'I'll do whatever you say.'

'You will?' He stood over her for a long time with his frozen smile, and behind the window stood the pines, calmly swaying in the breeze, and then the man suddenly held out his hand and with his fingers touched her neck. The woman shot to her feet; he saw fear and loathing in her eyes.

'Let's talk like grown-ups. I'm not going to do anything for nothing. You get me?' His tongue flicked over his lips. 'I wasn't talking about money.'

Staring him in the eyes, she began to back away, until she hit the giant, steel safe in the corner of the office.

'No,' she was shaking her head. 'No, no! This is some kind of terrible nightmare. No.'

'Let me be utterly frank with you. I can make him die. Today. Hang himself, for example. Or open his veins in the men's room, by the toilets. Would you like that kind of solution to your problem?'

'I'll take you to court.'

'Be my guest. You are very naïve, and you don't know anything about the law. You have no proof and you will never get any. And your Nikolai will be dead, and nothing and no one will be able to help him anymore.'

'This is vile!' She was trying to hold herself in check, speak firmly. 'It's despicable!'

'Words, just words. Today you say these things, but tomorrow you'll be thanking me. I won't let your husband out of here. And it will be your fault. You'll be doubly to blame – first for putting him in here, and then for not doing anything to help and save him. Well?'

She sat there crying, with her head bent down, clasping her face in her hands. Her bare shoulders trembled, and he could clearly see her bosom under her thin top trembling too.

'Well?' he repeated, but the woman didn't answer, and so he quickly came at her and pulled her towards the sofa next to the safe. With clumsy fingers the man struggled to unbutton her blouse, but the woman tried to break free and so he simply tore it open and the woman hit him and screamed, and the sofa's black leather was icy-cold and seemed sticky, and there behind the wall, in the waiting-room, the ageing secretary turned up the radio with a knowing smile and looked out of the window: a green colour, the colour of the forest, calms the nerves well, she thought to herself. An excellent therapeutic tool for people with frayed nerves. The telephone rang. The woman in the white coat let it ring a while and picked up the receiver.

'No, no, he's not in just now. Call back later. Ten, twenty minutes, I should think. Or better still, just to be sure, try again in about an hour. Good day.'

She carefully placed the receiver back. Order in everything, that was how she liked it.

MORNING

Bertrand came early in the morning, when everyone in the ward was still asleep.

Opening the door without a sound, he walked silently through the corridor, past the orderlies sleeping on the sofa. He paused in the middle of the ward, scanning the men on the beds and floor. When he spotted Nikolai on a mattress between two metal cots, he walked softly up to him. He bent down over him and lightly touched his shoulder. When Nikolai opened his eyes, he whispered, 'Get up. Quietly. Let's go,' then stood up again.

Still dazed with sleep, Nikolai sat up obediently and with weak hands began to put on the blue hospital shirt and trousers lying next to the mattress. From time to time he cast a glance at Bertrand.

Bertrand frowned, impatiently checking his watch.

***

The orderlies, pressed tight against one another, were still sleeping on the sofa. On the ground floor someone's beige raincoat was hanging on the coat rack by the door. Nodding towards it, Bertrand told Nikolai to put it on.

Bertrand opened the door and went out first, scouting the street. Nikolai waited in the hallway, having wrapped himself in the over-large coat.

Bertrand poked his head back inside. 'All clear, come on out.'

They walked for a long time along the endless hospital paths. Nikolai squinted. After the gloomy rooms and corridors where the thick opaque windows barely let in any natural light at all, the bright morning sun hurt his eyes. Their steps reverberated in the quiet morning air: Bertrand's firm and confident, and Nikolai's shuffling in his hospital slippers.

'Do you remember what day it is today?' asked Bertrand without turning back. Nikolai thought for a moment.

'It's the anniversary of my son's death. Five years.'

'Correct.'

Bertrand pulled out a pack of cigarettes and offered it to Nikolai. 'Smoke?'

As they walked Nikolai fumbled with the pack for a long time before he managed to take out a cigarette. Bertrand handed him his gold lighter. Nikolai stopped and shielded the lighter with his hands as he lit up; he had to jog to catch up with Bertrand again. Rounding the corner of the building, they saw a man watering the asphalt and lawns from a hose. He glanced at them fleetingly, then turned his back. They crossed to another, adjacent path, where bushes concealed Nikolai's rumpled hospital trousers and his misshapen, worn-out slippers.

They approached the wall. Bertrand slowed down, looking around, then abruptly grabbed Nikolai by the arm and dragged him with a jerk into the bushes.

'Take off the coat,' he ordered. Nikolai complied without a second thought, then Bertrand unfurled the coat and threw it up on the wall.

'There's glass up there, you could cut yourself.' He clasped his hands together to give Nikolai a leg up. 'Climb up, just be careful of the glass. And hurry!'

Without hesitation, Nikolai placed his foot on Bertrand's hands. Bertrand easily lifted him from the ground. He pushed himself off and fell forward onto the coat on top of the wall. As he scrambled to turn, he scraped himself on the jagged bottle shards which poked up from the concrete.

Bertrand watched from below.

Before he jumped, Nikolai turned his head and looked back into the hospital garden. The man they'd just passed was lying in the grass, arms outstretched. The hose, still pulsing with water, was wriggling next to the man like a living, shiny black snake. Its steely sharp tongue stabbed at the grass.

Nikolai wondered about the man while he was on the wall and while he was jumping off, pushing himself with his hands and chest off the concrete, but once on the ground he forgot everything, had no thoughts of anything at all. He picked up the raincoat from the grass, dusted it off and put it back on. Quickly, without looking around, he set off and ran along the road, soft with grey-blue dust, arms swaying, stooped forward, panting, stumbling on pot-holes, falling – yet as in a dream, without feeling any pain.

***

The hospital was in a pine grove beyond the outskirts of town. A passing truck gave him a lift, dropping him off very close to home. Nikolai jumped out of the cabin, forgetting to thank the driver, and began walking home, feeling more and more anxious. As he turned into his street he started running again, just like in the forest earlier. In the dark vestibule he pressed the button next to the elevator. The glass circle flashed red and the doors opened immediately. He rode up to the third floor. Once there, he rang the doorbell and stood listening for a long time, holding his breath. He had no key.

'Vera, open the door,' he said finally, in a penetrating voice.

He rang and rang the bell.

He had to make a decision: break down the door or climb up via the balconies? No, the balconies were a bad idea, he decided – it would give her enough time to hustle out her lovers then leave herself. He mustn't abandon the stairwell. He sat down on the stairs and pictured, smirking, the tumult he had unleashed inside the apartment: rats dashing from room to room, dressing hurriedly, trying to think how they could scurry away. But there was no way, no way in the world they could succeed, because he was here, right here by the door, where he could see everything. He even thought he could make out their hurried footsteps, their whispers, behind the door. He chuckled soundlessly; he had caught them all at once, like flies in a jar.

Suddenly he shot to his feet. What if they had decided to climb down the balconies themselves? How had he not thought of that before? He unbolted the stairwell window and poked his head outside: there was no one on their balcony. Like a complete idiot, he'd sat there on the stairs for at least ten minutes – easily enough time for them to have climbed down to the neighbours' second-floor balcony, knock on their window, explain their sudden appearance with a story of lost keys, a fire, any number of things, and then undisturbedly walk down the stairs and out of the door, entirely unseen. Nikolai looked down. His wife was walking from the flower shop to the park. She was dressed in black, carrying flowers in her hands.

THE CEMETERY

She walked quickly, head bowed, a black scarf covering her hair.

The first fallen leaves – yellowing but not yet dry enough to break into pieces – littered the asphalt under his feet. Occasionally she disappeared behind the trees, but quickening his step, Nikolai easily caught up with her. All that time the woman did not look back once.

The low graveyard wall began just beyond the park. One corner had been dismantled and a heap of grey stones lay in the grass. The woman took a narrow path to the wall, stopping for a moment next to an old beggar-woman.

The old woman gazed after her, bowing and crossing herself continuously.

Nikolai stood at the tree-line for a minute then went into the cemetery. Keeping low, he hurried towards the graves. An acrid stench of burned leather and plastic billowed over the cemetery. The keepers had spent the previous day gathering up and incinerating old wreaths. It was hot.

He was seen sitting in the grass among the graves. After a while no one took any notice.

***

Vera bent over the grave, pretending to cut the dead flowers and toss them into the grass outside the little iron graveside fence, but Nikolai, sitting just an arm's length from her, could see her surreptitiously glancing now and again over to the gap in the wall where the beggar-woman stood.

She was eager, excited...

It was hot. Without getting up, Nikolai took off his raincoat.

A heavy, small sun hung in a cloudless sky.

Nikolai didn't know what was supposed to happen next, nor what he was waiting for, seated among the graves in the lush cemetery grass. He had no thoughts at all, he was just watching the gap in the wall, watching Vera, all in black, her hair concealed beneath a headscarf. Every so often he looked up and stared into the sun, without squinting, and afterwards a little black sphere would dance across his eyes, obliterating everything.

The grave fence beside which Nikolai was sitting had been left unfinished, and in the grass lay a stack of flat-topped iron railing bars, bound at the ends with scraps of iron wire. Nikolai, exerting all his strength, heedless of the pain as the sharp ends of the wire bit deeply into his fingers, began to unwind them.

***

When he looked up at Vera again, she was no longer alone. She wore a shy, excited smile, and the flowers – dirty-brown like dried blood – fell slowly from her hands. Someone was walking through the little gate, his back to Nikolai. Nikolai could not see his face. He tugged hard at the wire one last time, and black, thick droplets of his blood fell onto the bars and the grass, which bent under the weight. Burning in the sun, they ran down to the ground, vanished...

Rising unsteadily to his feet, Nikolai saw the woman hold out her hand while the other kissed it, and this gesture seemed to go on forever, endlessly tormenting him. Nikolai saw how a hand brushed her cheek and moved lower, caressing her neck and shoulders; how Vera closed her eyes, and with a moan as quiet as a sigh pressed her frail, yielding body against him.

There was no need to stay hidden now, she would not see him.

Nikolai ran towards them, clutching the metal bar in his hand, black with blood.

***

He was seen sitting in the grass among the graves. After a while no one took any notice. No one saw the man jump suddenly to his feet and rush at the young black-clad woman tidying a child's small grave. In the man's hands was a heavy metal bar, a piece of railing with a flattened point. As they turned towards the sound of her scream, they saw only how the woman fell, and how the man, taking a swing, hit her prone body for the last time.

Then he dashed between the graves, as if he were chasing someone, shouting and lashing the air with his iron bar.

No one tried to stop him, or approached the woman lying motionless on the child's grave among the vivid asters. Riveted with horror, they watched silently, taking cover behind other graves. At last someone rushed off to find a telephone, looking back all the while and stumbling into grave-plot railings as he ran.

SERGEANT BERTRAND

After throwing away the bar, he went back to the woman. He stood over her for a long time, glancing indifferently at the crowd slowly gathering around him. The beggar-woman looked out from behind their backs, making the sign of the cross and mumbling to herself.

From the direction of the wall – not from the gap side – a man was walking up quickly and confidently, with long strides. No one noticed him until he was right next to the people standing in a circle around the grave. Without slowing, he continued towards the young man with the long scar across his brow that disappeared somewhere into his thick, blond hair; towards the young man who stood helplessly over the bloodied woman.

There was some movement, some near-imperceptible blow or something else. No one among the bystanders saw exactly what that tall, strong man did in the very moment that the murderer turned to him and reached for him, on the verge of weeping like a frightened child. And when he dropped to the ground, as though mown down, as though his legs had simply broken, the man bent down, lifting the woman easily in his arms as if she had no weight at all, then retreated quickly with the same firm, decisive tread past the people who in horror and revulsion parted before him; and soon, very soon he disappeared somewhere beyond the graves. One of them wanted to follow him, to help the man, and had already made a move, but where to go? There was no sign of him among the graves.

Over the cemetery hung the suffocating, bitter reek of burning leather, which seemed to have grown stronger. Beyond the wall there came the sound of a car approaching and pulling up, the clang of opening and slamming doors.

Everyone turned towards the wall.